THE BABY BLUE
RIP-OFF

THE BABY BLUE RIP-OFF

MAX ALLAN COLLINS

THOMAS & MERCER

Text copyright © 1983 by Max Allan Collins
Printed in the United States of America.

Published by Thomas & Mercer
P.O. Box 400818
Las Vegas, NV 89140

ISBN-13: 9781612185248
ISBN-10: 161218524X

This book is dedicated to my friend
Jan McRoberts 1948–1981

1

Something was wrong. I eased out of the van, shut the door as soundlessly as I could, and jogged up toward the house, leaving behind what I'd come to deliver. Because something was definitely wrong.

From half a mile down the road, I'd spotted the lights; every damn light in the house was going, which was way out of character for its occupant, an elderly woman who had pinched pennies for so many years it was second nature now to sit in the dark and save on electricity. Yet here the house was, lit up like Christmas, beacons of light streaking out the windows of the clapboard crackerbox and cutting through the night the way a movie projector cuts through a dark theater.

The next thing I noticed was the cars. Even before I'd brought the van to a halt, I noticed them, parked right up there next to the house, on the lawn, crowding the screened-in porch like relatives at a millionaire's deathbed. Actually, only one of the two vehicles was a car: a late-model white Pontiac GTO trimmed in sporty, tasteless red and blue—you could be arrested for desecrating the flag driving that car. The other vehicle was, like my Dodge, a van; only this one was a Ford and—unlike my relatively new, sky blue number—pale green and of indeterminate age.

The cars were just as wrong as the bright lights; the resident of the little bungalow didn't own any sort of car, let alone a GTO or a van, both of which seemed a little unlikely for an elderly, mostly incapacitated person. Why not a Harley-Davidson, or a submarine?

I was halfway up the lawn, feeling like a one-man task force invading some beachhead, when I started having second thoughts. Thoughts like maybe I was just letting the uneasiness of the day work on my mind. Maybe I was ready to expect the worst, after trudging through the sort of unpleasant, overcast day that migraine headaches were invented for.

The whole day had seemed out of sync, as if somebody had been shuffling the leaves of the calendar and a day got stuck in July that belonged in October. A cold, sullen day, with the night coming in before it was supposed to. It was dark already at seven o'clock, an hour that would normally be daylight-savings-time light. The temperature was fifty-seven shivery degrees on a date that would normally tally eighty-five or more.

I was walking now, not jogging, and I was maybe a hundred feet away from the house when I figured out what was going on. I did this by studying the dark figures moving around in the bright frames of light that were the windows of the little house. The figures were carrying things, lifting them. Taking them.

Stealing.

People in the house were looting it, cleaning it out. And as if gutting a house—any house—isn't bad enough, these lowlifes were preying on an elderly semi-invalid who happened to be a friend of mine.

Okay, I told myself, sucking in wind. Okay. Before you go looking for a tree and a vine to swing down into that house like Tarzan, maybe you better do your homework. I decided to get the license numbers of the car and van so I'd have that to hang onto in case I got the worst of the confrontation that was about to take place. Damn it.

Walking on eggs is the way you describe how carefully I was moving, and I moved that way around the back end of the patriotic GTO and zeroed in on the license plate. I'd been hoping it wouldn't be some deadly multi-digit that might overload my memory banks, and my wish came true: 70-3. Seventy was the county number; three was the vehicle number.

In addition to being easy to remember, the number told me something about the character of the GTO owner—or the three part did, anyway. It told me he was a lunatic. Because to get license plate number three, or any other early number, you have to be a pretty early number yourself. That is, you have to be at the Port City Courthouse bright and early the morning of the first day of license-plate sales, and that usually means camping out overnight on the lawn of the courthouse with a throng of fellow lunatics, all dedicated to the proposition that meaning in life can be achieved via the attainment of a low license-plate number.

Keeping in mind that I was dealing with at least one potential fruitcake, I moved quietly and carefully around to the back of the van, the rear doors of which were swung wide open. I had two unpleasant surprises. Let me list them in order of increasing disappointment: the van had no license plate at all; the van had someone in it.

Let me be specific.

The van had a big, hulking figure inside it, a featureless blob of darkness just one size smaller than the van itself. And I had just perceived the hulk as something not unlike a human being when it reached out skillet-size hands to fry me in. I heard my tee-shirt tear as the paws clutched at it and I was yanked inside the van. He'd been stacking things in there—the things he and his cohorts had been stealing—and I was just another thing to be hauled in and stacked. Only I got special, preferential treatment the inanimate objects didn't receive, though at the conclusion of that treatment I, too, might be an inanimate object.

What I'm trying to say is, he started hitting me.

They were backhands; he could've been fanning himself or swatting flies or something, but they sent me sailing just the same, tumbling onto one of his stacks, slamming into something—a TV I think—and when I stopped bouncing into things and felt the metallic surface of the floor, he kicked me in the side, gently, as if trying to put my ribs up my nose.

The next time the foot came down at me, I grabbed onto it and heaved up. Hulk went crashing awkwardly into the carefully stacked stuff in the van, a comical Frankenstein's monster smashing things he didn't mean to, and there was the appropriate noise to go with it: glass splintering, metal and wood scraping, even a bonging from an object that was apparently a grandfather clock on its side.

With Hulk helpless, I clearly had the upper hand, which I played to full advantage by scrambling the hell out of there, getting on my feet and heading back down the sloping grass.

Somebody caught me with a flying tackle, and I went down hard, the wind whooshing out of me and leaving me on the ground and rasping, gasping for air. Then I was surrounded by dark figures—four of them, maybe, or forty—and they began to beat on me. I covered my face and they hit me in the crotch. I covered up my crotch and they hit me in the face. It went on like that for a while.

When I came to, I was being dragged by the legs up the sloping lawn. My back was to the ground and I had a rather pleasant view of the sky, which had a lot of stars in it for the evening of an overcast day. My mind, however, was on other things—like feeling to see what was left of my sex life, and poking my tongue around my teeth to see if I'd be eating anything but baby food from now on. I couldn't see any of my captors and, quite honestly, I didn't try to. I was thinking about other things, like surviving.

As we approached the house, they dragged me like a squaw behind an Indian's pony (but with considerably less affection). My head went skipping over a stone, and I thought, giddy with pain, ain't that something; I'm the lake and the stone is skipping over me, and I skipped over another one and went away for a while.

I woke up inside the house. I knew that because there was a floor beneath me: a hard, varnished wood floor. It was dark in the house now. All those bright lights had been snuffed; it was so dark I could've been unconscious still, only my eyes were open. My first thought was: I'm alive. My second thought was: They're gone.

Alive, on my stomach on the floor in the house, alive; the lights off, so they've gone away, those men. Those men were gone now.

But they weren't.

The lights were off, and the robbing was over, but the robbers were still around. And they were talking.

About what to do with me.

"Tie him up?" A harsh whisper; gravel rattling around in a pan.

"Hell, no. Can't you see he's out of it?" A whine; Peter Lorre with no accent.

"I think we should off him." This was a new voice, no more pleasant than the other two. Chalk on a blackboard.

"What do you mean, off him?"

"Look over there and you'll know what I mean."

"Yeah. Damn. Maybe you're right. Damn. I see what you mean. Jesus."

"I say let's get the hell out of here. We ain't no godddamn killers."

"Is that right? Look over there and *see* if we ain't. There's an expert sitting over there who you could ask an opinion on that subject."

The voices were getting all jumbled up now. I couldn't tell who was who. I wondered, idly, which grating whisper belonged to license plate three; I wondered which was the big guy in the van. If he could talk at all. Maybe he was good at sign language.

"I say off the sucker—grease him and get out."

There was silence for a long, and I mean *long*, couple of minutes.

And then somebody came over and kicked me in the head.

The next time I came to, they *were* gone.

And I was alive.

I said it aloud: "I'm alive." I swallowed. I sat up. I groaned. I was alive, all right—messed up, but alive.

The argument about offing me must've come out in my favor, because I was breathing.

But somebody else in the room wasn't. I found a lamp and switched it on.

Somebody across the room from me, tied to a chair, was dead.

And suddenly there was dampness all over my face, and I felt the dampness with my fingertips to see if it was blood, and it wasn't. It was tears. I was bawling like a baby and didn't know it. Then I stopped, and I crawled over to the phone to get help.

2

It didn't start with people hurting other people, stealing from them, killing them. That came later. It started with kindness, the kindness of four old women.

But I suppose it started even before that.

With Sally.

Sally wasn't an old woman, and she wasn't much on kindness, either. What Sally was was young and slender and pretty, her hair natural blonde (that one I can swear to under oath) and her legs—to whom cellulite was a stranger—long and slender. Overall, there wasn't a thing wrong with Sally that a new personality wouldn't have cured.

She was the sort of woman who uses her good looks as a form of blackmail when she's in a good mood, and for revenge when she's in a bad one. Which didn't stop me from gratefully shacking up with her early that summer. Even if she did make me "share" the housework and cooking (meaning I did most of it). Sally was a liberated woman who did whatever *Ms.* magazine told her to, and I put up with all the emasculation quite cheerfully. We all have our masochistic moments, and in my case, remember, those moments were a prelude to long legs and natural blonde hair.

Sally isn't going to be in this story much longer, so I'll get to the point, which is that she worked at the local hospital as a dietician. She insisted the job at the hospital was "temporary," as she wasn't long for a little hick town of twenty thousand like Port City (she hailed from Burlington, after all)—and in fact wasn't going to be long at all for a little state like Iowa if she could help it. Mid-summer a job application came through for her, and she kept her word and is now in New Jersey somewhere, at another, bigger hospital, putting together menus for sick people.

But I'm getting ahead of myself.

Anyway, Sally was a dietician (pardon, *the* dietician; Sally would insist I make the distinction) at Port City General and was in the habit of frequently professing a belief in "getting involved." She only became a dietician, she said, because it enabled her to "help people, in my small way," though I didn't ever see her donating her sizable paycheck to cancer research or anything.

"Mallory," she said to me once, during foreplay, "do you have any idea why I decided to get involved with you?"

(See what I mean about Sally and "getting involved"? Shacked up is what we were.)

"Yes," I said, wilting. "I've often wondered why you chose to give yourself to an undeserving wretch like me. Just this second I was wondering that."

Sally didn't much care for sarcastic remarks, unless she was the one making them, so she pushed me away and said, with no sense of irony whatsoever, "Screw you, Mallory."

(Most persons of the female persuasion I've known—and I use "known" in several senses of the word, including biblical—have called me by the not unaffectionate diminutive "Mal." They will say, "Screw you, Mal." Not "Screw you, Mallory." I tend to take the latter as an insult, though I may be playing at semantics.)

"Are you ready to listen?" she said.

That meant, was I ready to shut up. I nodded.

"I chose you," she said, "because I thought you were an activist, like I am."

She voted straight Democratic.

"I chose you," she continued, "because you wear your hair rather long, by local standards, and of the men I've met in this lousy little town, you were the only one with long hair who wasn't a high school kid."

Ridiculous. First, my hair barely covered my ears, like an early Beatle. Second, even considering hair an issue, at this late date, branded Sally as the aging former hippie she was.

"Also," she continued, "the doctors at the hospital are too old for me and, frankly, much too conservative for my tastes."

The doctors were married.

"You, Mallory, are young."

Thirty. So was she. Which is why she liked to think of it as young, of course.

"And you have money in the bank and aren't just some grubby little leech wanting to suck up my paycheck."

Power to the people.

"Also, these conservative upright Port City types just aren't my cup of tea."

Her cup of tea was another kind of tea altogether.

"But you," she said, "you I thought were different. But no, you aren't, not at all. You're as conservative as the oldest old turd sitting on that bench in front of City Hall."

She liked to say words like "turd" to shock me. Shall we all blush together?

"You don't think you're conservative, Mallory? Oh, but you are. If you weren't conservative, Mallory, you'd get involved."

"How?"

There was my mistake. Right there. Opening my mouth. Asking a question. Mistake.

So she told me how to get involved, and I did.

I sure did.

But I must admit that the eventual depth of my involvement didn't have much to do with Sally. She's just the person who bumped into me, knocking me off a cliff; I mean, she didn't put the damn cliff there or anything—she just bumped into me.

You see, Sally is one of those persons for whom the term "lip service" was coined. (In more ways than one, but that's another story.) Sally got involved in politics, for example, by saying "Right on!" while watching her candidate speak on TV. Sally got involved in ecology by putting a litter bag in the front seat of her oil-burning Pontiac. Sally got involved in bettering race relations by calling blacks "black" instead of "Negro" and by making sure to invite one to every party she threw. You've met her.

So Sally's getting me involved was, initially, no great burden for me. And it was more worthwhile an involvement than the usual run of Sally's lip-service mill.

What Sally wanted of me was a vested interest of hers, meaning it related to her job as dietician at the hospital more than her sense of humanitarian purpose. I was to take hot meals around to four old people during the supper hour, one evening a week. The service was provided at a nominal fee by the hospital so that old folks in the community who were living alone would be sure to get at least one hot meal a day. When Sally explained that this was what she wanted me to do, because one of the volunteers in the service had had to drop out for the summer months, I was relieved and glad to do it.

I was one of several dozen people in Port City who had taken on this particular good deed. Doing it once a week was no big strain, especially since it was summer and I wasn't busy with a damn thing anyway, except taking a course in literature at the college two mornings a week and writing my latest mystery novel, which mostly ran to afternoons. I could spare the time.

There was only one irritating aspect to my getting involved with the hospital's Hot Supper Service (as it was ingeniously titled), and that was that by the time I had done my duty for the first time, Sally and I had broken up.

As I promised earlier, Sally isn't going to be in this story much longer, and I wouldn't even mention her if she hadn't been the prime mover for getting me into one of my larger messes, playing a peripheral Stan Laurel to my center-stage Oliver Hardy. And I think it's interesting, if irrelevant, to note how a person out on the sidelines of a certain chain of events can make so great a dent in those events without even trying.

As far as our breakup scene goes, I'm not going into detail about it. I didn't find her with another man; she didn't find me with another woman. (I didn't even find her with another woman, which would at least have been a change of pace.)

She just got tired of me.

And chose to tell me, of course, while we were in bed—and not sleeping, either; she had a bad habit of using that most inappropriate of occasions to bring up topics for discussion.

Well, I was tired, too, and told her so; told her we'd just been using each other, and a good time was had by all, but good-bye. And I moved back into my house trailer on East Hill.

But should you ever happen to pick up this book, Sally, keep reading; even though you aren't in it anymore, stick around.

See all the trouble you caused me.

3

The bad thing, I thought, about my getting involved in the Hot Supper Service was the flock of old people I'd be serving. Four of them; four old ladies. God forbid I'd be asked in to chat with one of the tottering old relics. Who in hell wanted to watch the decaying creatures gumming their food, saliva and masticated glop dribbling all over their hairy-warted chins? Yuck. I accepted the Hot Supper Service as a good thing, theoretically, being a humanitarian at heart; but, like so many humanitarians, I harbored a secret dislike for humanity. Old people, particularly.

For example: I'd see some old guy driving in a car in front of me, going thirty in a sixty-five zone, and I'd say, "Why don't they get those senile old bastards off the road?"

For example: I'd be in a hurry to get some money out of my bank account, and some old bag'd be ahead of me at the window, cashing her social security check and having the teller divide up the money and place it into envelopes marked "rent," "groceries," and so on, and I'd think, "Just pass away in your sleep, why don't you, and save yourself the trouble."

But I was signed on for the duration. So there I was in my blue Dodge van, setting out to feed the elderly multitudes, with four self-lidded Styrofoam plates of hot food sitting on the floor in back. I hadn't got around yet to carpeting and fixing the thing up, so my Styrofoam passengers got a rough ride.

The hour or so a week I had to spend delivering the meals took me all over Port City. As a rule, Hot Supper volunteers had a single neighborhood to service, but no such luck for me. Apparently I'd been saddled with a grab-bag list of leftovers from the other routes, giving me the Port City grand tour, starting with Mrs. Fox on West Hill.

West Hill is steep, rising out of the downtown business district, looking out over the bend of the Mississippi along which Port City nestles like a rhinestone in the navel of the land. The hill's view has been spoiled somewhat by the factories that crowd the river, cluttering the scenery and dirtying the water. None of that had particularly bothered the factory owners who built the luxurious gothic homes of West Hill, as they'd found that from their perch things looked sufficiently rosy, the distance blurring out unpleasantness the way a soft-focus camera does wonders for an aging movie queen. And many of those founders of local industry died before factories were considered eyesores, before the word pollution crept thoughtlessly into the national vocabulary; and these good city fathers left both wealth and a wealth of problems to their children. Those children, being from solid stock, rose to the challenge of the changing view from West Hill by moving into high-priced housing additions and condominiums, some of them in Port City.

Mrs. Fox, like the gray two-story nineteenth-century home she lived in, was a survivor of another time. The house had been a showplace once; now it was a paint-peeling, oversize embarrassment in a neighborhood still clinging to the vestiges of class.

The first night I delivered a meal to her, I had climbed the walk up the slanted, surprisingly well-kept lawn, feeling somewhat nervous. I half-expected to be met by an apparition, a

West Hill version of Gloria Swanson in a Port City Community Playhouse production of *Sunset Boulevard*.

But the door opened to reveal a petite woman with a smooth, wise, quite pretty face. Her cheekbones were strong and high, her hair white and pulled back in a discreet bun; only the looseness of the flesh under those strong cheekbones gave a hint of her age, which had to be seventy at the very least. She wore a simple blue cotton dress, with a white cameo brooch at the neck. She walked with a cane—because of arthritis, I found out later.

"Mrs. Fox?"

"Young man?"

"I'm here with your food. From the hospital?"

"Oh! The Hot Supper man! Come in, come in. What happened to that nice couple that was bringing the meals around?"

"I don't know, ma'am."

"No matter. Follow me, please."

She led me from the entryway into a large living room, where an oriental rug of oranges and yellows and reds, a baby grand piano, a fireplace, and assorted obviously antique Louis XVI furniture were dominated by a light wood ceiling carved in wonderfully graceful rococo detail.

"A German fellow did that," she said. "Many years ago. No one carves that way anymore."

"No," I said. "I don't suppose so."

Still awestruck by the room, I somehow managed to hand her the Styrofoam plate of food and watched with some surprise as she pulled a TV tray from somewhere, set it up in front of an expensive-looking old lounge chair, and put the plate on the tray. The tray was out of place in that room, like a man arriving at a costume ball a week early.

"Unlike most living rooms," she explained, smiling, "this one *is* lived in. The upstairs of the house is entirely closed off—has been for years—as is most of the downstairs; I only use the living room, kitchen, bedroom, and bath. Can I get you a lemonade, young man?"

I refused, and she went on to say, "Oh, I had so hoped I could connive some company out of you. This is a beautiful old house, but it's a bit lonely for one."

I explained to Mrs. Fox that I had three more stops to make on my route, but promised to make her last on my list the following week so I could stay and visit for a while. I kept my promise, and that next week she treated me to a memorable evening of reminiscences about earlier days in Port City. Seems her husband had been one of the men involved in initiating local pearl button manufacturing, which helped earn Port City the unofficial title "Pearl Button Capital of the World"; but in the days of plastic buttons, that came to mean little, and Mr. Fox had stubbornly clung to pearl when other Port City plants were converting to plastic. He had died bitter, and broken if not broke. Mrs. Fox felt lucky to still have the old house, one tangible memory of a more prosperous time.

"Our boy George, our only child George," she said, "runs the Allstate insurance office here in town. And George has tried to get me to let go of this old house, but I won't do it."

"I don't blame you."

"Oh, he's been good about it, considering. Comes over and does the lawn for me, and once a week his wife helps me clean the old place. That son of mine is why you're here tonight, young man, because he's the one who got me into this Hot Supper business. Said he was afraid I wasn't eating proper. And you know something? He was right. Kind of lonely cooking for one in that big drafty kitchen."

The thoughtful son was something of a running refrain along the old Hot Supper trail. Only in the case of the Cooper sisters, it was a thoughtful nephew.

The Cooper sisters were twins; whether they were identical twins or not, I couldn't tell you. They were similarly built, being graceful, willowy old gals who must've been lookers in their day. I tend to think they *were* identical twins, though, as they both looked much the same. But then so do most eighty-year-old women.

They lived on the bottom floor of a two-story house; the upper floor they rented out to some college students, who played very loud rock music up there. Neither sister seemed to mind. Or hear, for that matter. The house was a pleasant old yellow clapboard, hardly a match for Mrs. Fox's mansion on West Hill; just a sturdy, well-kept house in a neighborhood of similar houses. The neighborhood shared the valley between East and West Hills with the downtown area, a belt of churches and schools separating the business and residential districts.

The Cooper sisters had been living together for a long time—all their lives, I supposed—and probably in this same house; only in fairly recent years had they decided, for practical reasons (both monetary and physical), to rent out the upper floor, and to move all their furniture onto the lower floor. For that reason their living quarters tended to be cluttered; there were chairs enough to seat a meeting of the DAR, old photos of relatives and old paintings by relatives, tall cabinets brimming with china and bric-a-brac, and all the doilies and knickknacks in the world.

These sisters fit my stereotypical idea of old folks like round pegs in round holes; if I'd thought the intelligent and gracious Mrs. Fox was evidence of the fallacy of my downbeat thinking about the elderly, here was ample rebuttal.

Or so you might think.

Because the Cooper sisters proved me wrong. Just seeing the Cooper sisters showed me the error of my ways. Stay with me and you'll see what I mean.

Miss Gladys Cooper opened the door, with sister Miss Viola Cooper right behind.

"Why, Mr. Mallory," Miss Gladys Cooper said, "we haven't seen you for years, tell me ..."

"... what have you been doing since last we saw you?" Miss Viola Cooper said, picking up her sister's train.

I might as well come out and tell you that the Cooper sisters had been living together so long that they had become a single person, in a manner of speaking. Now I mean just that—in their manner of speaking, they were a single person. They thought so much alike, and each knew her sister's mind so well, that either could complete a sentence for the other, with neither noticing.

"Hello, Miss Cooper," I said. "Hello, Miss Cooper."

"Well, good evening, Mr. Mallory, and to what ..."

"... do we owe this unexpected, and rather overdue, visit?"

"I'm the Hot Supper delivery boy. See?" And I displayed the lidded plates in my hands.

"What happened to the Petersens?" Miss Gladys Cooper said. "They were such a nice young couple. But of course that doesn't mean ..."

"... we aren't delighted to see you again, after so long a time. Come in, come in."

I came in.

Miss Viola Cooper took the dinners into the adjacent dining room (most of the brimming china cabinets were in there) and readied the long table, while her sister questioned me.

"Well," I said, "I'm finishing up my four-year degree at the college, slowly but surely, on the GI Bill. I've traveled around some, and I'm trying to write freelance full-time now. I sold a mystery novel last year...."

"Yes," Miss Gladys Cooper said, "we've been following your career with interest—"

"And surprise," chimed in her sister from the dinner room. "You didn't show any particular literary bent when we first encountered you, you know."

"Not that you weren't one of our favorite students just the same," the other sister assured me.

That's right; the Cooper sisters had been teachers of mine. My second- and third-grade teachers, to be precise, and I loved them. Then and now.

But I hadn't seen them for a lot of years; in fact, the Cooper name on the Hot Supper list had rung no bells. Face to face, though, it was impossible not to know them.

They insisted I stay and have a glass of wine with them while they had their supper, and I stayed long enough for one glass (homemade dandelion wine, very nice) and begged off, promising them that two weeks from that night, I'd make them last on the route so I could visit all evening with them.

Which I did, and that was when they told me about their nephew David, who had enrolled them in the Hot Supper Service because he suspected that their nightly meal with occasional wine had lapsed into nightly wine with occasional meal.

My preconceptions about old people were changing fast.

That first night, when I'd been able to stay for just a few minutes, the sisters had left their meals midway to see me to the door.

"You were in my last group of students," Miss Gladys Cooper said, somewhat wistfully, "that final year before our retirement."

"You were in my second-to-last group of students," Miss Viola Cooper said, equally wistfully, "the year prior."

(I'll give you a moment to figure out which one taught second, and which one third.)

"You young people are wonderful," Miss Gladys Cooper said. "I don't know why so many older folks think so poorly of you."

"Like those lovely boys upstairs," Miss Viola Cooper said. "So sweet and so thoughtful, and why they're ..."

"... quiet as mice," her sister finished.

From the racket going on up there, the mice had to be wearing combat boots and into the Clash. But no matter.

"You know, Mr. Mallory," Miss Gladys Cooper said, "a lot of people—older people, I mean—have a stereotyped view of your age group."

Her sister nodded. "Just because some of you wear your hair a bit extreme and dress in unorthodox apparel at times, many of these elderly people think there's something wrong with you, the silly old fools."

"Silly old *ignorant* fools," Miss Gladys Cooper added. "And if you can remember back to our class, Mr. Mallory, 'the seeds of ignorance....'"

"... bear the fruit of prejudice,' " I finished.

"You remembered," Miss Viola Cooper said, smiling.

"Sort of," I said.

4

I reserved Mrs. Jonsen for last because her place was out on East Hill, not too far from where I live. East Hill is the grab bag of Port City. Older middle-class homes dominate, sedate two-story houses of brick and/or wood, with rundown areas stuck in this corner and that, with an occasional higher-class neighborhood sitting aloof to one side. And, too, you can find certain East Hill streets that seem designed to display the multitude of American life-styles like an exhibit at a World's Fair: a split-level home, relatively lavish, sits side by side with a cheap prefab; a handsome, well-preserved two-story gothic, dating back to when Mrs. Fox's digs were dug, shares the same side of the street with a tumbledown shack occupied by some wino.

Mrs. Jonsen lived on the outer edge of East Hill, just outside the city limits, on the corner where Grand Street turns into one highway intersecting another. Once upon a time, Mrs. Jonsen must've felt relatively safe from the madhouse that is East Hill. But we've crept in on her, largely due to the shopping center, car dealerships, discount department stores, chain restaurants, gas stations and such, which have come to line that edge of the city like so many plastic-and-glass tombstones.

Not that Mrs. Jonsen complained about the encroaching city—at least not in my presence, anyway. She wasn't a complainer, Mrs. Jonsen.

Matter of fact, if my negative feelings about the elderly hadn't been dispelled by the rest of my Hot Supper charges, Mrs. Jonsen would've done the trick all by her lonesome. Even if the other names on the list had belonged to gnarled, senile old coots, Mrs. Jonsen alone would've turned me around.

Because if my image of old people as grotesque, barely living artifacts was a stereotype, then Mrs. Jonsen provided the necessary counter-stereotype. She was the universal grandmother; a kind, apple-cheeked old lady with (God help me) twinkling blue eyes and warm, winning smile.

On the other hand, she turned out to be far less spry than the other oldies-but-goodies I'd met thus far in my campaign. Like Mrs. Fox, she had arthritis, only much worse; she was pretty badly crippled, both hands and feet, and used a steel walker to get around her small house.

The house was a modest, single-story gray affair that had once been used as quarters for the hired hand and his family on the Jonsen farm. Mrs. Jonsen's late husband had been a basically kind man (she said) but somewhat bigoted (she didn't say that; I just gathered it). He had known that the cheapest labor he could find for his farm would be "coloreds" and therefore chose to situate the hired hand's quarters on the far end of the farm, rather than the customary side-by-side arrangement.

This was only one of many interesting things Mrs. Jonsen told me that first night. She had been last on my list, and when she invited me to stay, I didn't refuse.

"I have some oatmeal cookies, fresh-baked," she said. "Would you care for a plate, young Mallory?"

Before Young Mallory could say don't go to any bother, she was going to bother. She struggled out to the kitchen on the metal walker, and I took the plate of cookies she brought me after her equally slow and awkward return trip. The cookies were, of course, very good. Grandmotherly good.

"You're wondering," she said, letting go of the walker and flopping down into a soft armchair, "why I'd bake cookies and yet have my meals delivered."

I admitted that that had occurred to me.

"Like to keep my hand in," she said. "Wouldn't mind cooking for myself, but Edward—that's my son—says cooking's too hard for me, what with my arthritis and all. D'you know Edward?"

"No, ma'am."

"Edward's a good boy, but I wish he'd get married, like his sister. But he's forty-eight now, so I doubt that he will. He's a nice-looking boy, but a bit plump. I guess I fed him too well as a child…. Well, my word, I forgot to bring you a glass of milk. What's wrong with this old woman."

"That's okay, I'm fine…."

"No, I insist."

She started to rise, clutching onto the walker, and I got up myself, saying, "I can find it," and went after the glass of milk.

Her kitchen was spacious—considering the size of the house—as big as her living room and remodeled fairly recently. Though the walls and ceiling were cream-colored, as were the counters and cabinets and appliances, the dominant color was blue. Two walls were completely covered with mounted blue plates, decorative plates that upon closer observation revealed Christmas scenes: sleighs, decorated trees, reindeer, candlelit churches, lots of snow—all the standard concepts dressed up somewhat differently on each plate in shades from dark to baby blue. There were eighty-some plates, and each was dated, starting back at 1895. The designs were simple but striking, and it was an impressive display. Christmas seemed to radiate out of the wall, even if it was late June.

"Oh, the Christmas plates," she said, when I returned milk-in-hand and mentioned them. "Our one extravagance." She laughed. "From what you've heard me say about my husband Elwood, you may have guessed that he was ... somewhat tight with a dollar?"

I nodded. I had indeed guessed that Elwood was tight with a dollar. He made Silas Marner look like Hugh Hefner. The only thing that might tie him to those Christmas plates was a kinship to Scrooge.

"Once a year ... at Christmastime, as you might guess ... Elwood would have one of his relatives in Denmark send over one of the plates, and that would be his special gift to me—special because it was not the practical sort of gift he'd usually give. Those plates aren't cheap, you know. About twenty-two dollars apiece they're up to now, if you send to Denmark—twice that in a store—and every year they break the mold, never make that particular plate again. Wouldn't be surprised if that collection of mine's valuable, as those things go. At least I know it means a lot to me, enough so's I kept it up since Elwood's passed on."

"They go back a long way."

"Elwood's mother, for a wedding present, gave me her plates. She'd collected them from the start, in 1895. We were married in 1919, and we haven't missed a plate since."

The rest of the living room was antique-heavy, too, and when I mentioned that, she said, "More of Elwood's mother's things; that cabinet of china over there, all very nice, very old pieces; that set of crystal goblets on the mantel is, too.... She left all her things to Elwood and me."

"She really collected some beautiful things."

Mrs. Jonsen laughed and said, "Elwood certainly didn't get his thrifty ways from his mother. Old Beth Jonsen spent her husband's money and enjoyed it, which is what Elwood and I should have done, I'm afraid. When he passed on, twenty years back, I sold the farm lock, stock, and barrel, just holding onto this little house and the piece of ground it's on. Used some of the money to fix the place up—spartan is the word for the way Elwood had it fixed up when the help lived here—and I gave a substantial portion of the rest of the funds to our boy Edward."

There was a pregnant silence, and I said, "What did Edward do with the money?"

"Bought himself a filling station. Let me tell you a story about that. Edward always has been a determined boy, a lot like his father—all the stubbornness, if not the tightness of money ... and though it's unkind to say so about one's own offspring, which you love very much, he just never had the horse sense his father had. How are the cookies holding out, young Mallory?"

"Fine."

"Plenty more."

"No, really."

"Where was I?"

"Edward always has been a determined boy."

"Oh yes, well, when Edward was just a youngster, he used to work at this certain filling station, pumping gas. My husband Elwood believed that a child had to earn his own way to appreciate the hardness of a dollar—and that was when a dollar was truly hard, remember—and so in addition to his farm chores, Edward went to work while he was still in junior high school, buying his own clothes and that sort of thing. Though in defense of my husband, we never made the boy pay room and board.... If you want more milk, just help yourself."

"Thanks, ma'am."

"Just go on out to the kitchen; this story'll hold."

"I don't care for any more."

"If you do, you know where it is. What was I saying?"

"Edward used to work at this filling station."

"Edward worked at this filling station, where he got a lot of abuse from his boss, a fellow name of Meeker who liked to treat his help like so much dirt. You can tell a lot about a person by the way he treats his help, you know. That Meeker fellow divorced his wife, too, to give you some indication of the man's character. As I was saying, Edward got it in his head that one day he would buy this Meeker out and own that station himself. And, well sir, determined boy that he was, he did. A lot of years went by first, of course, with Edward staying on at the farm and helping his father, but when Elwood came to his untimely early end, I gave Edward a substantial portion of the money we got for selling the farm, and he bought himself that filling station."

She smiled.

"And?" I said. "What happened after that?"

She frowned. "The station went broke that first year," she said. "Sure I can't get you another plate of oatmeal cookies? Plenty more, though I must save some for Edward. They're his favorite."

5

It was a month before I got back around to Mrs. Jonsen again. Oh, I saw her every Thursday evening, dropped off her Hot Supper all right. And promised her that as soon as possible, I'd make her last on my route again so we could have another chat.

Which was something I very much wanted to do; my prejudice against the aged had turned to fascination. These wonderful old ladies were memory books come to life, living, breathing bundles of the past, containing all the wisdom, folly, pain, pleasure, joy, sorrow of a lifetime. Talking to them, I felt a sense of nostalgia for days I'd never known.

But that next week was when I spent the evening hearing Mrs. Fox reminisce, and the week following was my night with the Cooper sisters, and the Thursday evening after that I had a poker game to go to, and so it was a month before I got back around to Mrs. Jonsen.

And too bad, too. Because that was that July evening I told you about; that July evening that seemed like October, where the van and the red-white-and-blue GTO were crowded around the porch of Mrs. Jonsen's overlit little house, and I made my feeble attempt to play hero and got kicked in the ribs (among other places) for my trouble.

So the second time I came to spend an evening with Mrs. Jonsen was the last time.

And she had nothing to say.

She was, after all, dead; tied to a chair in the kitchen where all those blue Christmas plates had hung. No more. Only faded circles where they had been—every plate, like much else in the house, was gone.

6

Sheriff Brennan took off his white Stetson and played with a lock of greased brown hair. He was wearing a red-and-blue hunting jacket, and under that the cream-colored shirt and cream-colored slacks that, along with the badge on his chest, made up his uniform. Brennan was well over six feet tall, a wide, solid-built man, with less paunch than most men his size, age, and disposition.

When he first came in, accompanied by his deputy Lou Brown, he was all business, and brusque but not offensive in his questioning. I had told him some of the details over the phone—I'd caught him, not a deputy, when I called—but he was taking it all down again, and some new stuff I hadn't got around to saying before, writing it all in a little notepad.

I told him I couldn't be sure how many of them there had been, but at least three and probably four. When I mentioned the red-white-and-blue GTO, license number three, Deputy Lou Brown chimed in, "That's Pat Nelson's car. He called it in stolen."

So much for remembering license-plate numbers.

Nonetheless, Brennan had called the local and state police to let them know about the GTO and the green van. He made several other phone calls, the first of which was to the coroner, and it was after that call that he sent Lou Brown out to the patrol car to get a camera for the coroner's dead-body pictures. Brown, who was about my age and an old high school acquaintance of mine, was a tall thin guy with black hair and a white complexion, extra white tonight. His pencil mustache and neatly trimmed sideburns looked especially black next to his pale, pale face.

After the initial questioning, Brennan said not a word to me, while he got everything in motion. But now that the situation was under control and the detail work beginning, Brennan was starting to get restless. He paced. He wandered around like a caged animal. He was simply too big a man for Mrs. Jonsen's little house; he was the freak show's giant stuck in the midget's dressing room. Restless, pacing, wandering around, Sheriff Brennan was getting pissed off, and that meant he'd be talking to me again.

You see, Brennan didn't like me much. And our mutual dislike was about all we had in common.

I was sitting on the arm of the couch in Mrs. Jonsen's living room. From where I was, I could see into the dining room, off to the right, beyond which was the kitchen, off to the left. The couch was one of a handful of things left in the room. The television was gone, along with the cabinet of antique china and some of the older, nicer pieces of furniture; most everything was gone. In addition, much that remained had been torn apart, as if looting the place wasn't enough and a finishing touch of vandalism had been necessary. Pillows and couch and chair cushions had been gutted by some sharp knife; even the flowered wallpaper had been chopped into here and there. The braid rug had been rolled carelessly to one side, and floorboards had been pried loose. Any furniture that didn't fit the category of antique had been knocked over, mostly broken by the force of the act.

Suddenly Brennan stopped pacing. He looked at me like he hadn't noticed I was there before. He said, "What're you doing here, Mallory?" He rocked back and forth on his feet.

I didn't say anything. He seemed to want me to be a smart-ass, so he could yell at me or maybe slap me around a little. But I didn't oblige him. I'm never witty after getting kicked in the nuts.

"What're you doing here?" he continued. "What's this delivery-boy horseshit?"

"It's just something I was doing."

"What were you delivering food at seven o'clock at night for?"

"I was about an hour behind schedule. I got to talking to one of the other old ladies."

Light flashed from the kitchen, where Lou Brown was taking pictures of the body. Brennan turned to go out to the kitchen and said, over his shoulder, "I'll be talking to you some more, Mallory."

"Terrific."

"You sit right there."

"And here I was planning to dance," I said, finally obliging him with the smart-ass remark he was after.

He stopped and looked at me hard. "Maybe you find this funny."

I stood. "Not at all, Brennan. It's just I'm bored with your stupid macho act, which is what you fall back on for lack of being able to launch an actual investigation." I was pointing a finger at him like a gun.

"Don't point your finger at me—"

I showed him another finger.

"Brennan!" It was Lou Brown, in the kitchen.

"Yeah, coming," Brennan said, glaring at me, then joining Brown.

I sat down.

More light flashed in the kitchen doorway. Two ambulance attendants came in, rolling a stretcher behind them. Brennan told them just a minute, and they stood outside the kitchen in the dining area, which was just as emptied and torn up as the living room. The attendants wore traditional white and seemed anxious to get in there, like guys on the bench waiting to get in the game. I wondered if they'd run the siren coming out here. I doubted they would run the siren going back.

A fat man in a brown suit burst through the front door. He was just short of being round; his flesh was doughy and paler than Deputy Brown's. His hair was the same color as his suit, and he was balding, combing his hair over the front of his head from in back where it was still growing, Zero Mostel–style. In fact, he resembled Zero Mostel, only not funny.

"Look at this place," he said, looking at it. "Oh my God, look at it." He peered into the living room and covered his face with a pudgy hand. "Jesus Christ, will you look at it! So much gone, so much ruined!"

He padded into the kitchen and the house seemed to tremble.

I heard him say, "She's dead?"

There was a mumbling that must've been Brennan or somebody saying, "That's right," or something. It wasn't a question that took much of an answer. It didn't take a doctor to pronounce *that* body dead.

"What can be done?" he said. He spoke loud. His voice was baritone, but not very masculine.

There was another mumbling: somebody saying, "Nothing can be done," or the equivalent. Maybe somebody said, "Bury her," which is about all you can do for a dead person, after all.

It was silent for a while.

Brennan waved the ambulance boys in, and some of the people in there (which ones I don't know, because I was still in the living room and couldn't see into the kitchen) got Mrs. Jonsen's remains untied from the chair and moved onto the stretcher. It was a slow process. Five minutes went by before the attendants passed through the dining room with the covered stretcher. The fat man in the brown suit followed along behind them like a pallbearer. Brennan closed the door after the fat man and the ambulance attendants.

No siren.

"Who was that?" I said, knowing.

"The son."

"Edward Jonsen?"

"Edward Jonsen."

"Isn't there a married sister?"

"Lives out of town. Not contacted yet."

"Oh. He sure seemed upset. About the house, that is."

"People react funny in these situations. What do you know about it anyway, Mallory?" Brennan said that, and then his face flushed, as he remembered I had lost both my parents in recent years. "Sorry," he mumbled.

"Why was this place torn up, Brennan?"

"I don't know. Add insult to injury, I guess. Looking for something, maybe. Buried treasure. The Jonsens had a reputation for being hoarders, stingy, that sort of thing. Who knows? Now I want you out of here, Mallory."

"I thought you wanted to talk."

"You thinking about getting involved in this, Mallory?"

That phrase again. *Getting involved.* Damn.

"What if I am?" As if I wasn't.

"Just don't. You used to be a cop once, I hear. Now you're a big mystery writer, with a book coming out one of these days. Maybe you want some publicity. Forget about it."

"Can I ask you one thing?"

"No."

"Can you find the people that did this?"

"I don't think that's your concern."

"Oh, it's my concern. For one thing, I knew the woman they killed. She was a friend of mine. For another thing, those sons of bitches kicked me more than any man should ever have to get kicked. And one last thing, Brennan—I'm a taxpayer and you work for *me*; I pay your goddamn salary, so don't tell *me* it's not my concern."

I guess I expected my little speech to get a rise out of Brennan, but he disappointed me.

Because my outburst had cooled him down, if anything, and he touched my shoulder in a fatherly way that would've angered me if it hadn't been sincere. "Let's not bitch at each other," he said. "Tonight you think you're the detective in your book. Tomorrow morning you're going to know better."

"Answer my question, Brennan."

"I don't know, Mallory. I can tell you some about it tomorrow. Come talk to me. Can you wait till then?"

"I guess."

"How you feeling?"

"Bruised. In every way imaginable."

"Will you go on over to the hospital and get looked over? I'll call them at Receiving and tell 'em you're on your way."

"That's not necessary...."

"Yes, it is. Get checked over."

"Well. Okay."

"Feel up to driving there yourself? I'd like Lou to stick here with me awhile, or I'd have him drive you."

"I can manage."

"You take it easy, Mallory."

"Yeah. You too, Brennan. Uh, sorry I...."

"Yeah, I know. We shouldn't be bitching at each other right now. There's a woman dead, and that's more important than how we feel about each other."

For once I agreed with him.

7

No great excitement had been stirred at the hospital by Brennan's call that I was coming. A nurse glanced at me, saw that my head and limbs were still connected to my body, and said, "Have a seat." I had one. I had one for about half an hour before the doctor came around.

The pin on his white tunic said "Jameson." Jameson was sandy-haired, around thirty, and of medium height. He had brown-rimmed glasses over eyes that never looked at you, even when they did. He seemed bored.

"How are we feeling?" he said.

"So-so."

"What have we had happen?"

"We were kicked in the nuts, and just about everywhere else."

So he took us into an examining room, and we took off our pants. We coughed to the left and to the right while cold fingers poked. Then we sat on a cold steel table and were probed some more, all over. Occasionally we said ouch.

After a while the probing stopped. "We'd better have some X-rays taken."

"Okay."

"Can we have them taken tomorrow morning at nine? The X-ray technician will be on duty then."

"What's the problem anyway?"

More probing. "Some broken ribs, perhaps."

"How many?"

"We won't know for sure until we've had an X-ray. Awfully sensitive on the right side, and some ribs could well be broken. Or maybe just cracked."

"I see."

"You can pay at the desk."

He was gone.

I knew there'd be a catch. *We* got examined, but *I* paid.

Which I did, at the desk, after getting back into my pants. As I was putting my lightened billfold back in my hip pocket, Lou Brown walked into the lobby. The deputy was as pale as ever and looked vaguely upset.

"Buy you some coffee, Mallory?"

I said okay and followed him into the hospital coffee shop. It was about 8:55 and they closed at nine, so we got dirty looks from the waitress to go with the coffee. I ordered a sandwich, too, and got a look so dirty I almost lost my appetite.

But the coffee was hot and good, and it came right away. Lou sipped his and said, "How you feeling, Mallory?"

"I've had better nights."

"Me too. This is the first murder I ever worked."

So that was why he seemed upset.

I said, "How long you been a deputy, Lou?"

"About eight months."

There generally aren't more than one or two murders a year in a small town like Port City, and when there is one, it's the city police who handle it. This particular murder fell in the sheriff's domain because it had occurred outside the city limits and was therefore county business.

"Well, Lou, in your job, you got to expect to come onto a crime of violence now and then."

"Oh, it's not that. I seen blood before. We've had plenty of accidents to cover, and hell, I was an MP in the service—saw some rough goddamn things. But never this. Never an old woman beat up and killed."

"Is it pretty definite she was beaten?"

"I don't know. Too early for any official word. But it looked that way to me."

I nodded. "That was my impression, too. She wasn't bloody or bruised, but her hair and clothes were all mussed up, and I just had the feeling she'd been slapped around before she died."

"Heart attack, probably. You know, Mal, when I was taking those pictures of her, I kind of studied her, tied there in the chair, and I could almost see what happened to her. Guys asking her where she kept some damn thing and slapping her to make her tell, and her heart just gives way. Crazy thing is, these goddamn guys probably never intended killing her, just meant to tie her up and sack the place. Damn."

"Damn," I agreed. "What's up, Lou? Why aren't you still with Brennan?"

"Through for the night. Heading home. Brennan just said to stop here on my way and see how you were."

"I'm touched at his concern."

Brown grinned. "Yeah, what's the deal? Do you two hate each other, or what?"

"We're not sure ourselves."

"The way you were yelling at each other back at that house, I'd think you hated each other's guts. Then after a while there, you were talking real civil."

"Well, I got a certain amount of respect for Brennan. Within his limitations, he's a good sheriff. Except when he's looking out for the interests of his political buddies and various other string-pullers around town."

"I kind of gathered there was some friction between you two because of his son John. I remember how thick you guys were back in high school."

"John and me went back even before that, to junior high. Even then I was always smart-mouthing Brennan, and Brennan never did like that. Not that I blame him."

"You and John went in the army together, didn't you?"

"That's right. The Buddy Plan, or whatever the hell it was called. And John died, and I lived, and Brennan's resented me ever since."

"That simple, huh."

"Well, not really. After I got out, I was one of the Vietnam vets against the war. Pretty active. Brennan got wind of that, and I've been a traitor ever since. He thinks this is still the sixties and I'm a hippie who thinks cops are 'pigs' or something. It's sad, really."

"Weren't you a cop yourself at one time?"

"Yeah, a very short time," I said, and told him how I'd been on the force for around six months in a small California town a few years ago. And that I'd worked for Per Mar, a security outfit in the nearby Quad Cities, for a while. Then we got sidetracked, with me mentioning how for the better part of five years I'd been outside Port City, doing this and that, finally coming back to roost and taking a shot at writing; and Lou mentioned he'd been gone for several years, too, working in a factory in Ohio. Anyway, we got sidetracked, and it was along about this time that the waitress told us to leave because it was fifteen minutes past the coffee shop's closing and she had a right to go home like anybody else.

Out in the hospital lobby, Lou said, "You thinking about playing cop, Mal?"

"What do you mean?"

"You're involved, aren't you?"

"Don't say that."

"Well, you *are*. Involved in a murder. You were beaten up, and besides, you were a friend of the old lady's, weren't you?"

"Tell me the truth, Lou. Did Brennan put you up to this? To find out my attitude?"

"No. I'm just curious."

I shrugged again. "I don't know what the hell I'm going to do. If you and Brennan can take care of this, fine. But I admit I'm pretty pissed off about the whole thing, and wouldn't mind getting my hands on the SOBs responsible."

Lou just nodded.

"See you, Lou. Come over to my place sometime. I'll see if I can't find a beer for you."

"I'd like that. I could use a place to get away to."

"Love to have you. Is there a problem?"

"Well, I'm living with my folks, and it's driving me crazy. I'm trying to find an apartment, but till I do, I'm stuck with the folks, and I love 'em, but they drive me goddamn crazy. A twenty-nine-year-old man does not belong in his parents' home."

"I agree. Only on holidays."

"And Christmas is a long ways off."

We chatted for a few minutes more, and just as we were starting to part company, Lou said, "Almost forgot the reason I came looking for you. Was supposed to find out how you were, to tell Brennan. What's your condition, anyway?"

"Got my ribs messed up a little. Maybe cracked, maybe broken."

"Damn. Does it hurt?"

"Only when I breathe."

Lou went off to call Brennan, and I headed out to the parking lot and got in my van.

For a moment I thought about what Lou had said, about my "being involved."

No way. Let Lou and Brennan handle it. Like Brennan said, in the morning I'll be over it.

I started up the engine, turned my head, and glanced out the rear van window to back out of the parking space. My eye caught something on the floor. Something white.

A Styrofoam plate.

Mrs. Jonsen's supper.

8

My house trailer sits way back from the street in the middle of a big green lawn. On a dark night you can't even see the trailer—that is, assuming the streetlight directly in front of my place is not shining, and it usually isn't. One of my neighbors (the guy in the split-level) has his ten-year-old son shoot out the streetlight with a beebee gun so that, come nightfall, my trailer will fall into what the neighborhood thinks is a well-deserved obscurity.

This was one of those nights. The streetlight wasn't going, and as I pulled up to the curb, just getting back from the hospital, it was so dark that I thought for a moment somebody had hauled my trailer away.

I love my trailer.

It is very old—one of the oldest existing house trailers anywhere—a long, silver, faintly phallic module, plopped down in the center of a big luxurious green lawn like something laid by a dog from outer space. On one side of me is that split-level I told you about; on the other is a two-story with very nice gothic lines—and well kept up, too, I might add. You might wonder what a house trailer is doing on that big luxurious green lawn between those two high-class dwellings. I already explained that East Hill is a study in contrast, but my trailer next to the homes that bookend it makes the rest of East Hill seem normal.

The story is this. Several years ago there was a big hole where my big lawn now resides. That hole was a neighborhood eyesore, a dump of sorts, filled with weeds and dead trees and debris, and the city took steps to do something about it. They purchased the hole and sold it to a firm who used it as an experimental landfill project. The hole was then filled with garbage, the garbage having been dunked, like a doughnut, in various chemicals, and some dirt was put over that. Nobody wanted to live on the former hole. Nobody wanted to walk on it, let alone build on it, for fear of sinking into the garbage. Which is why I was able to rent the former hole, cheap, and put my trailer on it.

Considering the entertainment value, I don't see what the neighbors are complaining about, really. Many of them spend their spare time watching me and my trailer, perhaps in the hope they'll see us go sinking down into the hole like the *Titanic*.

Anyway, the streetlight was out, most probably due to my neighbor's little sharpshooter. I climbed out of the van, walked up toward the battered hull I call home, began to unlock the door, and somebody put an arm around my throat.

I was not expecting that.

I was not expecting to be attacked a second time in just a few hours. The bastards could have had the decency to wait till tomorrow, at least. But decency they were short of.

The guy with his arm around my throat told me to come around behind the trailer with him, where we couldn't be seen from the street. I did that.

There were more people than just the one. So far they had stayed behind me, but I heard them walking, breathing, felt them there. Maybe just two of them this time. But more than one.

Once in back of the trailer, I was given a forearm across my shoulder blades that sent me flopping on the ground like a professional wrestler faking a fall. If he'd hit me much harder, I just might've made my neighbors happy and gone sinking down to garbage level.

Somebody stepped on the back of my neck. I ate dirt for a while. It didn't taste good.

"Mallory," a voice said.

It was a harsh, whispering voice; I didn't recognize it, exactly, but felt sure it was one of those I'd heard at Mrs. Jonsen's.

"We wanted you to know something," the voice went on. "We wanted you to know we know you. We know who you are and where you are, and we don't want to see you again."

I lifted my face a shade—not far, considering the foot was still on the back of my neck. I said, "Can I say something?" My voice was rather muffled, since I had a mouthful of dirt.

"Go ahead."

"You guys are real morons coming around here."

Another voice. "We let you say something, and that's what you say? Jesus."

"Kick him in the ass."

Somebody kicked me in the ass. The shoe connected with my tail bone and rearranged my spine a little.

"We figure you don't know who we are, Mallory. If we thought you knew who we are, we'd blow your goddamn head off. Do you know that?"

I didn't say anything. Nobody can say I never learn my lesson.

"We're responsible people, Mallory. We aren't crazy. We didn't mean to kill that old woman. We were just ripping her off, is all we were doing. And anyway, she was old, man. Maybe she'd've died of a heart attack about then, anyway. Without our help. Who knows."

The other voice said, "Let's get out of here."

"Just a second. Mallory ... Mallory, be a good boy. Stay away from us."

"He doesn't know who we are; come on, let's get outa here."

"Mallory, don't try to find us. Don't come looking to figure out who we are. Don't try to be a hero again, like you did back at the old lady's place. Or you know what?"

He seemed to want me to speak, so I said, "What?"

"Or we'll kill you. That's what. Kill you."

"Yeah, we'll kill you, asshole."

And here's the good part: they kicked me.

In the ribs.

9

The next morning was hot. That brief flash of October in the middle of July had gone away somewhere, and I woke up to sweat-dampened sheets and got the air conditioner going even before I brushed my teeth.

It didn't take long to cool down the little trailer. My quarters were small, but very nice; the previous owner of the old trailer had been as attached to the thing as I was and had taken the time and expense to remodel the interior, putting in dark paneling and a fairly modern kitchenette. The living room was crowded by the possessions that make life bearable: a nineteen-inch Sony TV, stereo tape components, brick-and-board bookcase full of paperbacks, and walls bearing posters from several of my favorite movies: *Vertigo*, *American Graffiti*, *Chinatown*, *Goldfinger*, *Caddyshack*, and so on. I used to have the Penthouse Pet of the Year on one wall, life-size, but too many discussions about my possible status as a sexist were, shall we say, aroused by her presence.

By the time I had some clothes on, my ribs had started to flare up. I won't bother trying to describe the pain. It hurt. I didn't cry, but I thought about it.

At ten o'clock I was in the hospital coffee shop having breakfast; at ten-thirty I was getting X-rayed; and at eleven-thirty I was being told my ribs (two of them, on the right) were cracked, not broken—which was good news—and was strapped into a harness—which wasn't. If a girdle and a truss got together and had a kid, that harness would've been it. By noon I was pulling my van up in front of the courthouse, across the street from which is the jail. Brennan's offices are in the front part of the jailhouse, a big light-stone, two-story building that didn't look like a jail, really, except for the barred and caged windows and electrically fenced-in backyard, where the prisoners got their daily exercise.

Brennan was brown-bagging it in his office, studying some folders at his desk. It was cool—all the offices were centrally air-conditioned, unlike the jail cells—a pine-paneled cubicle with pictures of ducks on the wall, and some framed newspaper notices of Brennan's big murder case, where a local woman killed her husband with a pair of scissors and Brennan had caught her red-handed, you should excuse the expression. The woman is now serving sandwiches at Katie's, up the street, since husband-killing is generally considered justifiable homicide. There was also a color photo in a gold frame on his desk: his son John in uniform.

Evidently our temporary truce was still on, as Brennan treated me to a Pepsi, tossing me some change and telling me to help myself from the hall machine and bring him one, too. I did, then broke the truce by telling him, for the first time, about my return visit from the rib-kickers the night before.

"Jesus Christ, man!" he sputtered, getting some Pepsi on himself. He jerked up into a sitting position and, seeing as he'd been leaning back with his feet on his desk, that took some maneuvering. "Why the hell didn't you call us?"

"I'd had pain-in-the-ass enough for one evening."

"Bullshit!"

"Use your head. What the hell would've been the point of bothering you guys again? When they kicked me, I blacked out for a while ... a couple minutes, at least. By the time you could've got to my place, they'd have been long, long gone."

That calmed him down, sounded reasonable to him. He put his feet back up on his desk and said, "Christ. We just can't have people going around doing things like this."

"Kicking me in the ribs, you mean? I agree."

"Screw your ribs. I'm talking about looting houses, and now, killing people." Brennan gestured to a folder on his desk, next to his sack lunch. "Take a look."

I did. There were clippings from the *Port City Journal* dating back to April, the first good weather. Seven other homes had been similarly emptied. I'd remembered the rash of breaking-and-enterings, but for some reason hadn't tied it up to Mrs. Jonsen's. Maybe because some aspects of the other robberies didn't exactly fit the Jonsen one, as Brennan was soon to point out.

"Seven goddamn house lootings," Brennan said, "in four goddamn months, and now another one. Only this one don't exactly fit the MO of the other jobs."

"MO? Brennan, don't tell me you've been watching *Chips* reruns again."

"Look, prior to this job, the homes were left untouched ... all valuables gone, yes, but none of this vandalism crap. The whole damn Jonsen house was torn up, like some drunken kids out on prom night got together and whooped it up."

"Like you said last night, maybe they were looking for the fabled Jonsen money."

"Yeah. Maybe. Or maybe it's a different bunch responsible. Somebody who pulled this, figuring we'd tie it to those others." He made a face. "Glance at those clippings one more time, Mallory. Notice any common denominator?"

I skimmed them again. "Sure. All seven times the houses were where people weren't home. Either out for the evening, or out of town on some trip or something."

"Right, and that's another dissimilarity between the Jonsen job and the other ones."

I swigged my Pepsi. "Consider this. Suppose these people had some source of information that dried up. Suppose this job was either based on some new source of information, or was a first effort without that sort of help."

"How do you mean?"

"Well, let's say this group of rip-off artists had some way they've been spotting which houses are going to be vacant. One of them works at the gas or electric company, maybe, as a meter man, say, and has knowledge of who's going to be out of town for a while, or just overhears plans of going out for the evening when he checks the meter. Or maybe one of them has a girl friend who works as a secretary at a travel agency and knows who's on vacation. Maybe one of them works at the newspaper and knows who's having their papers stopped for a while. Or the phone company, and knows who's having phone service temporarily stopped. A lot of maybes like that."

Brennan had been nodding all through what I said. He said, "We've considered those. They sound good, until you knock 'em up against this job. Why would these people change their pattern now?"

I shrugged. "Could be they just thought someone would get wise to their present source of information. Could be that source got fired or laid off from that information-packed inside job."

"Or," Brennan said, "could be they heard about Mrs. Jonsen's supposed money and figured one old woman wouldn't be any sweat."

"Well?"

"Well what?"

"She wasn't, was she?"

"No. She sure wasn't."

We sat and looked at each other for a minute or so.

Then I got up, and Brennan stood.

"Thanks for talking, sheriff."

"It's okay. Thanks for letting me bounce some ideas off your head."

"Any time."

"Just one thing, Mallory ... don't let it go any further than just me and you chatting, okay? You can come around and trade theories all you want, but don't go nosing around."

"Wouldn't think of it."

"Mallory...."

"I said I wouldn't think of it."

"Bullshit."

"Hey, and we been so cordial up to now."

"Get the hell out of here," he said, trying to get gruff again and not quite pulling it off.

I headed for the door, and he stopped me.

"Say, Mallory?"

"Yeah, Brennan?"

He glanced at John's picture in the gold frame.

Then he said, "Never mind. See you around."

"See you around."

10

A big expensive Buick, last year's model, was parked in front of my place when I got back. The Buick was dark green and smaller than a yacht, but not much. A fat man's car. Appropriately enough, Edward Jonsen was in it. The car's engine was running, the windows up, air conditioning going. Even so, Jonsen was hot. Psychologically, if not physically. He was making an effort to contain his anger, but like a lid on a boiling pot of water, the attempt was not entirely successful; his lower lip took on a petulant jut and gave him the look of some talking animal in a cartoon, a pouting porker in a two-hundred-buck blue suit.

Jonsen was parked in my spot, so I left my van across the street, in front of the home of one of my friendlier neighbors. I crossed to the Buick and rapped on the window. Jonsen flashed a mean irritated look and pushed something, and the window on my side went down a third of the way.

"You're Mallory."

It wasn't exactly a statement; it wasn't exactly a question. I answered him anyway. I said I was Mallory.

"I have to talk to you. Get in."

He made no try at clouding the edge of hostility in his voice. I didn't know what to make of him.

I said, "We could go inside my trailer there and talk, if you'd like."

"The car will do fine, thank you."

He said thank you like screw you.

I hesitated.

"Will you get in?"

I nodded yes, and the window slid back up.

And so I got in. It was more than just cool in there; it was cold, uncomfortably so. In the backseat of the Buick were stacks of brochures put out by the feed company Jonsen worked for. After his flop at running his own service station, his mother had told me, Edward Jonsen had taken a job as a salesman for a big local feed company, and had evidently done fairly well, probably due to his farm background, which must've made it easy for him to relate to rural feed dealers.

Even now, you could see he'd been raised on a farm. His hands, which gripped the steering wheel as if he were driving and not sitting still, were hard, rough, callused, powerful. Hands that had worked. Hands that could do you damage. And yet the overall impression he gave was one of softness; the strength that obviously resided in his massively framed body was layered with the tissue of obesity.

"I'd like to express my sympathy for your loss," I said. "Your mother was a fine woman. I was happy to know her, even if it was only for a short time."

"Spare me your hypocrisy."

His jowls quivered as he spoke, the doughy, paste-white skin and the Zero Mostel hair making him an all-around unpleasant-looking human being. I wondered how the hell he could make a living as a salesman.

"I don't follow you," I said. "What do you mean, hypocrisy?"

"My mother's death *is* a great loss to me. But I was brought up to accept reality and the defeat it occasionally brings, so if you are attempting to mislead me by your pretended ignorance, or are simply hoping to needle me, I suggest you give it up." There was a firmness in his words and expression that belied the soft, almost feminine tone of his voice.

"I want to know what you mean by hypocrisy, Mr. Jonsen."

"*Please*. Although I have been able to accept my mother's death, the burden is still heavy, and I would as soon dispense with pretense and the sarcasm I detect in your tone. Coming to you like this is not easy for me. The whole idea of having to meet with you is distasteful, disgusting to me."

"What are you talking about?" There were goose pimples forming on my arms—whether from the air conditioner blasting at me or the chilliness of the conversation, I couldn't tell you.

"Let's not play games. Please! If you will return what was stolen, it can end there. I will even offer a cash settlement, though I'm sure it won't be as generous as some, well, fence, or whoever it is you usually deal with...."

"Wait a minute. What do you mean, 'return what was stolen'? I don't like your implication, Mr. Jonsen."

"Implication? Are you going to make me go through the chain of thought that led me to you? Please. Do you really think I'm naive enough to believe that a person of your ... *type* ... would participate in a program for aiding the elderly out of, what? Civic duty? Please. You used it as a method to get close to my mother, to get inside the house and see just exactly what it was she had in there. You were good, I'll admit that. When my mother spoke of you to me so highly, it didn't at the time occur to me that your motives were selfish. But now, with mother dead and everything stolen, it's easy enough to see. No, I don't believe your 'innocent bystander' story, and perhaps if, when I next speak with Sheriff Brennan, I explain my line of reasoning to him, he will see through your silly story as well. So why don't we drop the game-playing and talk seriously."

"You are incredible."

"The sum I have in mind is five thousand dollars. Hardly spectacular, I grant you, but if we were to agree to have the stolen property 'discovered,' then some of the intensity of the investigation might die down, which you will agree is to your advantage—"

"Can I get in a word?"

"Go ahead."

"I just want to point out a couple of things. Okay? Jonsen, don't assume that, just because you are petty, everyone else in the world is petty, too. And don't assume that, just because you are self-centered, everyone else in the world shares your warped point of view. Don't assume that, just because you have greed where other people have a vestige or two of compassion, the whole world is full of fat, greedy assholes."

"Is that all?"

"No. Get your fat ass, your fat car, and your skinny character the hell out of here, and don't come around bothering me again."

With remarkable speed, he reached down to the side of his seat, by the driver's door, and came up with a revolver. It was a tiny gun, a .22, and looked like a child's toy in the middle of his big hand. If I were James Bond, I would've laughed at it. I didn't laugh.

"Did you expect me to come unprepared?" he asked. "I realize who I'm dealing with. A murderer. A thief. I realize what you did to my mother, and I'm prepared to overlook that if we can make some kind of business arrangement, but don't underestimate me. I'm prepared to deal with you on your own low level."

"I'm sure you are," I said.

"Are you ready to talk seriously?"

"Sure."

He loosened his grip on the gun, lowered it, and I reached over and plucked it out of his hands. A tiny gasp escaped his lips: a child's gasp to go along with the toylike gun. His eyes were round white marbles as he looked at me pointing the little revolver back at him.

I let him sweat for a while; he could stand to lose some weight.

Then I tossed the gun in his lap.

"You didn't deserve her," I said.

He didn't know what I was talking about. He said so.

"Your mother," I explained. "And come to think of it, she didn't deserve you, either. Good-bye, Jonsen."

I got out, slammed the door, and the Buick roared off. I stood watching the empty street for a good minute, watching his exhaust fumes dissipate, then headed back inside my trailer and popped the top of a Pabst to wash the bad taste out of my mouth.

I sat on the couch.

Kicking me isn't enough, I thought. Now people got to come 'round and point guns at me.

Damn!

This really wasn't my idea of a good time, not to mention that I'd cut my lit class at the college this morning to talk to Brennan, and I had a mystery novel to write, and besides, it was time I got out and started looking for somebody to bandage my various wounds. Somebody soft who smelled better than me.

But *damn!*

Somebody had to care about Mrs. Jonsen's murder, and it sure as hell wasn't going to be her fat, spoiled son. *Somebody* had to care about her death. Not her damn possessions: her *death*.

Somebody had to (damnit) get involved.

Maybe it had to be me.

I finished the beer and started another.

11

Knocking.

There was a knocking at the door. I opened my eyes, slowly, tentatively, like a guy peeking into an envelope that just might contain his pink slip.

Beer cans.

I saw beer cans on the coffee table. I was on the couch, where I'd fallen asleep after consuming five beers while trying to think, an impossible task.

"Just a second," I told the knocking, or tried to. My voice was a fog of phlegm. I cleared my throat, tried again, and did better.

I got up and my legs seemed to work, so I answered the door. It was Lou Brown, dressed in civvies: gray tee-shirt and blue jeans. The light from outside did a number on my eyes, which I covered, reacting much as Count Dracula might.

"Did I disturb you?" Lou wanted to know.

"No," I said, without conviction. "Come on in."

"I should've called first."

"Hell with that. Hell with formalities."

"Are you awake?"

"Is a bear Catholic? Does the Pope crap in the woods?"

Lou laughed and said, "I'll come back some other time."

I laughed and said, "The hell you will. Come on in and talk to me. We'll have some beer, if I didn't drink it all. What time is it?"

"About four," he said, following me inside the trailer and closing the door behind him.

"Sit down. Be with you in a second; my bladder's killing me."

"Justifiable homicide," Lou said, noting the table of beer cans.

When I came back from the john, I got a couple Pabsts out of the fridge, popped the tops, joined Lou on the couch, gave him his beer, and started mine.

"What d'you do, Mal? Sleep all afternoon, or drink all afternoon?"

"First drink," I explained, "then sleep."

"That how you while away the hours? Drinking yourself unconscious?"

"It is till I figure out a way to drink and sleep at the same time."

"Can I ask you something personal? We aren't exactly close friends but is that all right, if I ask you something?"

"Go ahead, Lou. Maybe if I answer a personal question, we'll become close friends. Or maybe I'll toss your butt out of here. Who knows?"

He grinned at that and shot his best shot: "Are you able to support yourself writing? You go out to the college, too, I know. But you don't have a job."

"This may come as a shock to some people, but writing's a job. Not a living, maybe, but a job."

"Then how…?"

"When my folks died a few years back, they left me some cash. Not much … but I got some left. Enough to try to get a writing career off the ground. And the government pays my tuition. I'm an ex-GI, you know."

"Aren't we all? Your folks were in farming, weren't they?"

"Yeah. My father had a farm. There was some money there."

"I don't mean to be nosy."

"No, that's okay. I understand what it is you're doing, and it doesn't bother me."

"Oh? What is it I'm doing, then?"

"You're fishing around to see if maybe I might be part of that looting crew myself."

"Come on, Mal…."

"No, it's okay. Really. Doesn't bother me. I'm a natural suspect." Just ask Edward Jonsen.

"Listen, Mal, I won't deny it. It was just something I felt I had to touch on. For my own peace of mind."

"Forget it."

"Good," he sighed, relieved. "I'm glad you're not pissed. Because, actually, I was hoping to escape my folks for the rest of the afternoon, and hoped you wouldn't mind my hanging around awhile."

"Not at all. Glad for the company. Any time. But can I ask something in return?"

"What's that?"

"I give you refuge from your parents; you keep me filled in on Brennan's handling of the Jonsen case."

"What do you want to know? I thought you were going around to see Brennan this morning."

"I did, and I got *some* information, but I didn't want to press him. If he knows I'm planning to look into this, he'll clam up on me, and turn hard-ass."

"Then you *are* going to do some nosing around on your own?"

"Well, I don't know, exactly. We'll see."

"That sounds like yes to me."

"I don't know. People keep telling me I shouldn't get into this, so naturally I'm inclined to. You hear what happened last night?"

"Something else happen last night?"

"Yeah, I told Brennan this morning, but then, this being your day off, you wouldn't've heard about it."

"So what happened?"

I gave him a brief account of my visit from the Kick-Mallory-in-the-Ribs Club, and he shook his head, saying, "Those guys got balls, coming around here. The morons."

"Easy," I said. "That's what I said that got 'em started kicking again."

"How the hell *are* your ribs anyway?"

I lifted my shirt like a sailor showing off his new tattoo and let Lou see my girdled, trussed-up rib cage.

"Is that uncomfortable?"

"No," I said. "No worse than swimming in an iron lung."

"And you're still interested in playing detective? You got balls yourself, Mallory."

"Don't mention balls either," I said. "That's the other place those boys like to kick. Hey, I'm in swell shape. If I got invited to an orgy tonight, I'd have to man the punch bowl, I'm telling you."

"Listen, before I go into what I know about the Jonsen case, and the other break-ins, maybe you better fill me in on what Brennan told you so far."

I did, and then Lou went on to tell me some things Brennan had left out.

"Brennan's trying real hard on this one," he said. "He knows reelection's coming up, and he's been sheriff for a long time and knows people are in a house-cleaning mood around here, ever since the county treasurer absconded with God-knows-how-much."

"So Brennan's trying hard. So what?"

"Well, if he wasn't trying to make it a one-man show, he could call in the boys from the Iowa Criminal Bureau of Investigation, and that would probably result in a faster and more efficient clearing up of the case, but he's not going to, he says, unless he gets convinced he can't handle it himself."

"Great. And everybody knows how up-to-date Brennan is on police techniques."

"Don't underestimate him. He goes to Omaha to a three-week catch-up school for sheriffs every summer, and he says he picks up a lot there."

"He probably means women."

"That isn't what he means—"

"I'm just kidding, Lou. Go on, will you?"

"Okay. You get surly when you're drunk, don't you?"

"I'm not drunk, and I'm not surly, smart-ass. You want another beer?"

"Okay."

I got some more beers, and Lou went on. "Something else about the break-ins you might like to think about."

"Oh? What's that?"

"All of 'em took place beyond the city limits. Annexation got defeated at the polls last fall, remember? There's plenty of houses that extend past the actual limits, and all the break-ins have been among those."

"Yeah? Damn, I should've noticed that. Has Brennan?"

"I mentioned it to him, and he shrugged it off. Said it was just that those houses are mostly spread far apart from other houses and are easier to pull a van up to without rousing suspicion of neighbors."

"He's right," I said. "Those houses are on highways, too, mostly, where cars are going by too fast to take time to notice anything."

Lou nodded and said, "He's right, yeah, but I see more of a tie-in than just that. Outside the city limits means the sheriff's department handles it; inside means the local cops. Or some in town, some out means a combined investigation. I think staying outside town proper has to do with these people being afraid of what our police chief might do if he got into the fray."

"Oh, Lou, are you kidding? That fat nincompoop wouldn't do a damn thing."

"That's just it. The chief wouldn't do a damn thing himself, but he *would* call in the Criminal Bureau of Investigation. He always does in a murder case. He did about those rapes last year, remember?"

"And Brennan's not much for calling in the CBI."

"No. Like I said, he likes to fool around with a case himself, especially in an election year."

"And you think these B-and-E artists are sophisticated enough to consider that angle?"

"Why not? Besides, they're obviously local people and would've known that just from living in town and paying attention."

"I don't know. I live in town and I didn't know that."

"Maybe you're not paying attention."

"Keep that up and you won't get another beer. Listen, Lou, why is it obvious they're local people? Why can't they be out of Davenport or Rock Island or some place, and drive down now and then for a hit?"

"Mallory. You aren't thinking. And you who used to be a cop yourself."

"I still don't get you."

"I figured it from what you told me about last night—them coming back."

I thought for a moment, then said, "Damn! What's wrong with me? Of course they're local! They *knew* me! They knew where to look for me…. They wanted me to know that; to know they would come around and work me over if I caused them any trouble. And anybody who wasn't local would've split right after the job, would've headed back for wherever it was they worked out of. Lou, what about that car, that red-white-and-blue GTO?"

"License number three? What about it? You heard me last night when I said it was stolen, didn't you?"

I nodded. "But who was it you said the car belonged to? It was somebody I know…."

"Car belongs to Pat Nelson. You remember Pat, don't you? Went to school with us, a little ahead of us."

"I remember him. Had a run-in with him once."

"Oh?"

"That's neither here nor there, but did you ever consider Nelson could've been in on the robbery and reported his car stolen because he knew it'd been seen there?"

"After the fact, you mean? No, he called it in earlier than that, a good hour before you saw that car at Jonsen's."

"I don't know. I still think it could stand some looking into. Nelson's been in trouble ever since he was a kid."

"True enough," Lou agreed. "Reform school when he was barely in his teens, if I recall."

"That's right. You going to look into it?"

"Probably. Are you?"

"Probably."

"You want to do it together, Mal?"

"That's what I'd like, but we better work separately, or Brennan might cause us some headaches. We can just keep each other up on what we're doing."

Lou nodded.

"What ever happened to Nelson?" I asked. "I mean, what's he been up to lately?"

"Think he has a job with that silo company down in South End. He's married, you know."

"Who to?"

Lou grinned. "Don't tell me I'm the first to break it to you."

"Break what to me?"

"He's married to your old girl friend. Debbie Lee. Only she's Debbie Nelson now. They got a kid, I think."

"Yeah, right," I said. "I just didn't figure that marriage would've lasted this long." I shook my head. "Debbie Lee. Been a long time since I thought about her. My old flame."

"That dates back a ways, doesn't it?"

"Hell, yes. My first love. Junior high. *American Bandstand* and going steady and dances Friday night at the YWCA. Jesus, I haven't thought about those days in years."

"Well, neither has she, I'd bet. You ought to look her up."

"No," I said, "no, I don't think so. Married women tend to have husbands."

At this point the conversation drifted into other areas, mostly concerned with briefing each other on what we and friends of ours had been up to in recent years. At five-thirty I talked Lou into staying around for supper and while he called home to tell his folks, I got a couple steaks and some fries together, his share of which he wolfed down gratefully. Lou was pretty ragged from living at home. "You can love your parents without liking them," is the way he explained the situation to me.

At seven Lou and I were watching an old rerun of *Star Trek* when the phone rang. I answered it.

"Is this Mallory?" A female voice. Soft.

I said it was me.

"Mal? Can I see you? I have to see you."

"Who is this?"

"Debbie. Remember? Debbie Lee ... Nelson now. Can I see you? I can be over in ten minutes."

I held the receiver out and looked at it for a second. Then I shrugged, brought it back, and said, "Okay."

She hung up.

So did I.

"Who was that?" Lou said.

"You wouldn't even believe it," I said.

I showed him the door.

12

I was thirteen when I fell for Debbie Lee. It happened at a sock hop after school in the gym at the junior high. In certain obscure areas in Iowa hinterlands, this bizarre ritual is still practiced.

Debbie was just an inch short of five feet tall and looked like something her parents might've won at a high-class carnival: heart-shaped face, enormous blue eyes, appropriate Kewpie lips, cap of curly blonde hair, the living doll cliché come to life.

Also, she was cuddly looking, just a trifle plump (baby fat), and she wore pink a lot. Especially fuzzy pink sweaters. And even at thirteen she could fill a sweater out, one of maybe ten girls in the whole seventh grade who could. I think that was what was so appealing about her, really; not only did she look like the sort of picture-book princess a thirteen-year-old boy could worship with knightlike purity and devotion, but she was also the stuff wet dreams are made of, the possessor of a body designed to further madden an already puberty-deranged adolescent.

I expressed my love for Debbie, at that first junior high sock hop, by asking her for each slow dance; she accepted every time, and we would dance to the strains of "Wonderland by Night" or "Blue on Blue" (the only two slow tunes in the record collection of the acned fat kid who emceed every hop). It was heaven! Here I was, holding Debbie Lee in my arms (sort of—you could've driven a truck between us, actually)—though I wouldn't dream of hanging onto her like the "steadies" in the eighth grade who, rumor had it, "made out" frequently.... Well, I would *dream* of it, but I wouldn't dare try it. We didn't say a word to each other— "yes," "no," and "thanks" all being communicated by nods of the head—but nevertheless, true love it was, and I had optimistic enough an outlook to hope Debbie shared my feelings.

This, of course, is where the go-between comes in. Every junior high love story has a go-between. Our go-between, Debbie's and mine, was a girl named Darla whose complexion looked like the surface of the moon. Her hair was a ghastly reddish fright wig, her nose a beak, her eyes beady, her teeth buck. She was not attractive.

Which is what being a go-between is all about. The go-between is a girl who can't get a boy to save her life, so she becomes the best friend of an attractive girl and serves a function somewhere between agent and pimp, getting far more than her ten percent of the boy's attention. In fact, the boy will spend much more time talking to the go-between than to his actual girl friend. At least that's the way it was back in those days before the first shot of the sexual revolution had been fired. In my case, I went steady and broke up with Debbie Lee three times before ever saying a word to her.

It went this way: I would tell the go-between, Darla, how I felt about Debbie. Debbie would tell go-between Darla how she, Debbie, felt about me. And go-between Darla would tell both of us whatever the hell she felt like telling us.

And so, after an evening of slow dancing together at the YWCA, Debbie would give me a sorrowful look and would return my silver friendship ring. Immediately I would rush to Darla to find out why. Darla would explain that I had insulted

Debbie, somehow or other. I would plead my case to Darla, who would resolutely promise to do her best for me with Debbie.

The go-between's prestige depends on getting the best boy possible for her client, and therefore a schmuck like me didn't stand much of a chance with a cute girl like Debbie and a shrewd go-between like Darla. Soon I was seeing Debbie's round blue eyes staring woefully at me from across the gym floor while some older guy (an eighth-grader) would approach her and ask for a slow dance, and the vampire Darla would be sitting smugly in the corner, a smile of vicarious pleasure on her homely face.

Fortunately, Darla moved away that next summer, and in the eighth grade I made a comeback with Debbie, who was working freelance now. We even spoke occasionally.

And then disaster: Debbie became part of a crowd of "popular" girls who served as go-betweens for each other. A closed shop. This fleet of go-betweens was even more depressing than Darla, as they had boyfriends of their own and were in the go-between business for the sheer, sadistic hell of it. Talking to six of them during one day about the current state of Debbie Lee was like getting six different and equally upsetting opinions from doctors examining something malignant. By the time I was in the ninth grade, I had gone steady and broken up with Debbie Lee no less than sixteen times, investing in three rings (two wore out—swear to God) and having very little direct communication ... though we had taken to talking to each other on the phone every once in a while, usually in the presence of some go-between who was staying the night with Debbie and was constantly on the extension phone, giggling in.

Most frustrating of all was the fact that I had never kissed Debbie, in sixteen rounds of going steady. We'd never lasted long enough at one crack to get that far. And, since boys in the ninth grade are incredibly horny, something had to give.

What gave was that I took up with Debbie's best friend, a lass named Maureen who had a 38-24-36 figure (at fourteen!) and an IQ considerably smaller. Maureen put out (which means she let me kiss her and give her a moderate grope now and then) and, being Debbie's best friend, Maureen naturally told Debbie all.

I began getting irate phone calls from Debbie, wanting to know why I had never tried any of this kissing and groping stuff with her. Hadn't she, Debbie, been attractive enough to stimulate such activities on my part? I assured her I would be glad to do those things with her, but I was going with Maureen right now; I stood firm, because true love with Debbie was one thing, but groping 38-24-36 (at fourteen!) was something else again.

Gradually Debbie began to drop further hints that she was interested in me again. She broke up with her current boyfriend: a sophomore in high school, no less, with a car of his own. She accompanied Maureen and me to dances and movies, her blue eyes on me all the time, full of sorrow and longing. In a darkened movie theater, Debbie would grasp my hand; in the gym at the ninth-grade party, she'd ask me on a ladies' choice and would snuggle close till we were cheek to cheek, among other things. I took the hints and broke up with the luscious Maureen, who promptly took up with Debbie's sophomore. Free again, I made my intentions known to Debbie.

Who wanted nothing whatever to do with me now.

Of course.

Until a year later, in high school, when I had a car of my own. That got her interested again, and I asked her out on a date: homecoming. I offered her my class ring at the dance after the game, she accepted, and it looked like tonight would be the night—I'd kiss Debbie Lee at last!

And then on our way out of the dance, as I waited outside the restrooms while Debbie powdered her nose or something, a short, tough, red-headed upperclassman cornered me. He was, as fate's sick sense of humor would have it, a distant cousin of Darla, the go-between who moved away.

He said, "Pat Nelson's back in town." He had perfected a way of talking without moving his lips.

"Really?" I said. Politely.

"You know who Pat Nelson is, don't you?"

I knew who Pat Nelson was. Pat Nelson was a hood (pro-nounced like "who" with a "d" on the end), and I wanted noth-ing to do with him or his friends. Pat Nelson had been caught stealing sports equipment from the locker room at the junior high several years before, and had recently stolen a television set from a church. He'd been spending most of his time lately at Eldora, a reformatory for "wayward youths." Pat Nelson was pretty damn wayward, if you asked me.

"I know Pat," I said. "Pat's a good guy."

"That's right," the upperclassman said defensively. "Pat's a *hell* of a good guy, and don't forget it. And don't forget some-thing else…. He don't like it when guys go messing with his girl."

"I don't blame him," I said. "I wouldn't want anybody mess-ing with my girl."

"Don't be cute. Me and some other friends of Pat's seen you with her tonight."

Panic.

"Oh?" I said.

He prodded me with a finger attached to a short, beefy arm; his gray tee-shirt had full moons of sweat under both. "Stay away from his girl, if you know what's good for you."

What a corny line! I couldn't believe this guy! I would've laughed in his face if I hadn't been scared shitless.

"Pat's got a knife," he said.

"Good … good for Pat."

"What did you say?"

"Nothing."

"I thought you maybe said something."

"No. What's Pat doing home? I thought he was at Eldora."

"He's got good conduct leave."

"Oh."

"And he's back in town to stick his knife in anybody who messes with his girl."

"Who," I asked, knowing, "is Pat Nelson's girl?"

"Be reasonable, Mal," Debbie said later as I dropped her off at her folks'. "Pat's a nice boy, misunderstood. I felt sorry for him, so I wrote him a few letters, that's all."

I didn't see Debbie anymore after that. I loved her, but her sympathy for underdogs had gotten out of hand. I decided not to go out with girls who wrote to guys at Eldora who came home on good conduct leave with knives.

She went steady with Pat Nelson all through high school. She used to be in classes with me sometimes; she'd give me meaningful looks with those big baby blues, and I'd hurt inside from wanting to return them. Once I did, and a friend of Pat Nelson's (he was big on go-betweens himself) told me to stay the hell away from his woman. (Somewhere between sophomore and junior year in high school, the ownership term for females

71

shifted from "girl" to "woman.") I left Debbie alone after that, because I had a feeling Pat and Pat's go-between had gotten the information that I had exchanged meaningful looks with Debbie from Debbie herself. I began, as I got older, to consider Debbie a troublemaker, and spent the rest of my high school days in the company of girls who were easier to get a kiss out of, and whose previous beaux were nonviolent sorts, who carried nary a pocketknife.

But I never loved any of them like I loved Debbie. You never do, you know. You never love again as you do at thirteen, with so super-charged a combination of idealized adoration and puberty-stirred lust. Once your face clears up, the complexion of love changes too.

I should've kept that in mind when Debbie Nelson née Lee called me up and wanted to come over.

13

I gargled. Used some sweet-smelling concoction that was designed more to perfume bad breath than to cure sore throats or kill germs. But that was okay; perfumed breath was what I was after. Scent of peppermints and posies beats out that of belched beer any old day.

I grinned at myself in the bathroom mirror. Frowned. My teeth couldn't be *that* yellow. I brushed my teeth several times, grinned again: no improvement.

I sniffed under my arms. Bad news! I whipped off the frayed, cut-off sweatshirt I was wearing, stuffed it in the clothes hamper, climbed out of my rib brace and abandoned it as if faith-healed, soaped my underarms, and sprayed them with Right Guard. I walked to the bedroom to look for a shirt that might be a shade more suave than the frayed relic I'd been wearing. Unfortunately, owning no suave shirts whatever, all I managed to come up with was a bland cream short-sleeve number, but it had a collar and was pressed, so that was something. I got into it and looked at myself in the full-length mirror behind the bedroom door. I didn't look like Ronald Colman, but then, who does anymore?

I tidied the trailer. Got all the beer cans picked up and thrown away. It occurred to me that I'd had a hell of a lot of beer this afternoon, and that maybe that accounted for my light-headedness.

But in reality, I knew my feeling light-headed didn't have a damn thing to do with beer. It had to do with Debbie Lee coming over. The light-headedness had started then: when Debbie Lee (I mean Nelson) called up and said she was coming over.

I finished tidying the trailer, emptied ashtrays, vacuumed the front room carpet, straightened the books in my brick-and-board bookcase. Then I sat down on the couch. My living quarters and myself were all slicked up. Like a first date. My heart was pounding, adrenalin surging, and I felt like a damn fool.

Which I was.

Worse, I knew it. It's one thing to be a damn fool and unaware, and quite another to be a damn fool, know it, and go idiotically along being one. For instance, I *knew* this house-cleaning and instant revamping of me and my life-style was a silly, half-assed thing to do. As if I still carried the torch for Debbie after all these years! Even if I did still care about her in some cobwebbed corner of my mind, I cared about a person who didn't exist anymore, right? Yet here I was, sprucing myself up like I expected her to be just the same, a cute little blonde, with big blue eyes, in a fuzzy pink sweater. Hell! She was a housewife, with a kid eleven years old! She wasn't the thirteen-year-old storybook princess. She was a housewife and a mother, and thirty just like I was.

The doorbell.

I answered it, prepared for the shock of what a decade or so might've done to Debbie Lee.

Standing there, in the doorway, was a cute little blonde, with big blue eyes, in a fuzzy pink sweater.

"Debbie," I said.

"Mal," she said.

Violins played in my mind; surf crashed against mental beaches.

"Come in," I said.

"Thank you, Mal," she said. She came in.

I offered her a spot on the couch and she took it, crossing her short but shapely legs. She was the same. Or seemed to be at first glance anyway. Admittedly, the lighting in my trailer isn't much better than your average bar and may have put her into a sort of soft focus. Yet there she was: just as cute. She'd never grown any taller, of course; still just under five-foot. She wasn't dainty, though, but full-bodied and slightly layered with, well, I guess you couldn't rightly call it "baby fat" anymore. But if ever the phrase "pleasantly plump" was appropriate, it was now.

"You've changed, Mal," she said. "You look different."

"Longer hair," I said. "A little heavier."

"It looks good on you," she said. "Both the hair and the weight. You were skinny before."

"I'm also older, Debbie."

She smiled. A tiny smile. "Everybody is."

Then I noticed it; she'd frozen herself in time. She'd purposely stayed the same. People do that sometimes, you know, especially in small towns like Port City—they think of their youth (their junior high and high school days) as the best time of their lives, and they stay the same, or try to. They don't vary their fashions as much as the rest of us; Debbie still wore fuzzy pink sweaters, and her pink cotton skirt was a short shift that was decidedly out of style. And they don't change the way they wear their hair; Debbie still had the cute skullcap of blonde curls. She had never been much for makeup, having rosy cheeks and deep pink lips anyway, thanks to God or somebody being in a good mood when she was assembled. Overall, she had been much more successful in holding onto her youthful identity than most people who try. You should see the women with beehive hairdos running around the streets of Port City in pedal pushers like it was still 1960. None of them have heard of the B-52s, either.

"Listen," I said, feeling awkward, "can I get you a beer?"

"I don't want to be any bother."

"Bother? Hey, I'm glad to have you. I, uh, always wanted to look you up, but...."

"Yes. I know what you mean, Mal."

This was ridiculous! Here we were, talking in veiled, elliptical language, exchanging meaningful glances, as if we had shared some deep relationship. As if the last time we'd been together was at Casablanca, and not high school homecoming.

"Can I get you that beer, then?"

"Please."

I got two Pabsts from the icebox, gave her one, and joined her on the couch.

"You said it was important, Debbie, on the phone. You said you *had* to see me. You seem pretty calm now."

She smiled again. That tiny smile was the only one she had, but it was a dandy. "Maybe I'm being silly. When I called you, I was upset, but ... I've had time to think, driving over here, and now I wonder if I should've come."

"What's bothering you?"

"It's my husband ... Pat." She looked down at the beer in her hands. Her hands were small—very small—and white, and in the dim trailer lighting they looked like something carved in marble by a first-rate sculptor.

"What about your husband?"

"Maybe you didn't know that Pat and I ... well ... we're separated. Have been for several months now."

"No, I didn't know that." In spite of myself, I felt fireworks going off in my inner recesses somewhere. Celebration was in order.

"Pat has a drinking problem, of sorts."

"He's an alcoholic, you mean?"

"No. Not as I understand the word anyway. He isn't somebody who drinks all the time, gets up in the morning and reaches for a bottle. Not that at all. He'll go out maybe twice a week. Rarely more. Five days a week he won't touch a drop, not even a beer like we're having."

"Then what's the problem?"

"He ... when he does drink, he gets mean. He drinks himself silly and comes home and ..." She looked down again, for just a moment. She looked up, and her eyes were bluer than anything I'd ever seen. The best-looking sky on the clearest sunny day came in second to those eyes. "Mal, I know we ... haven't seen each other, haven't talked in years ... but I feel like you're someone I can trust, someone I can come to for help. I don't have many places to turn for help, you know. With Dad gone...." She got a little choked up and stopped talking for a moment. I got up and brought her a Kleenex and she dabbed her eyes.

Her father had died several years ago. He was a fine old guy, but both he and Debbie's mother were on in years when Debbie came along. Debbie had been a change-of-life baby, as a matter of fact, and her parents had been more like grandparents than parents to her. Her dad had died at sixty-eight and her mother, who was still living, must've been in her mid-sixties or older. Debbie had a brother, but he was much older than she was and had moved away years before.

"Go on," I said. "Finish about Pat."

"Well, I've … said it all, really. He just comes home drunk and gets mean. He's never hurt Cindy—that's our daughter—but he doesn't have much hesitation about … about beating on me."

And she started to cry.

More Kleenex.

My stomach was fluttering. Debbie had never been the emotional type when I'd dated her. I'd gotten to think of her as rather cold-hearted and manipulative, toward the end of our going-steady era, and seeing her break down, like a real human being, was disturbing.

"And that's why you came here?" I said after a while. "You wanted to talk to somebody about Pat, and this problem of his?"

"No," she said, stiffening her upper lip, taking a few final dabs with the latest Kleenex. She sipped her beer, smiled, and said, "No, that's why we separated. And divorce is only a few tiny steps away. I can see no hope for reconciliation, especially now…. I wanted to try, for Cindy's sake, but…."

"What do you mean, 'especially now'?"

"That's why I'm here, Mal. I got a phone call from Pat. Just before I called you. He was drunk … roaring. He said he was going to beat the hell out of me. And you."

"Me?"

"Yes. He had some crazy story about you trying to frame him for that murder. The one mentioned on the radio this morning—the old woman?"

The evening paper wasn't out yet, so she (and the rest of the town) wouldn't know the details as yet.

I nodded.

"You did find the old woman, didn't you? I heard that much on the radio. You did find the body and contact the police?"

"Well, it was the sheriff's department I contacted, but yeah, I did all that."

"Pat says you told … I thought he said police, but maybe he just said 'cops,' which could just as easy be the sheriff's people, right?"

"Right."

"Anyway, Pat says you told the cops or whoever that you saw his car there. He says you're trying to get this murder pinned on him. He thinks…." She smiled again, but at the same time her eyes teared up. "… he thinks you and I are seeing each other, having an affair, and have cooked up this scheme to get at him."

"Oh Christ!"

"It sounds crazy, I know. I can't believe Pat will still believe that when he's sober, but right now I don't think being reasonable is high on his list."

"No, I don't suppose so. And he says he's going to beat hell out of both of us?"

She nodded.

"Maybe we should call the police," I suggested.

"No!" she said. "I couldn't stand the embarrassment. He is … Cindy's father, after all."

"Okay. I can understand your point of view. But where do we go from here?"

"Is it true? Did you report his car as being at the old woman's place?"

"It's true," I said. "And it *was* there. But Pat is clear; he reported the car stolen, prior to the murder. So I don't see where he's in much danger of getting framed."

"He said something about that, too. Mumbled something about maybe you did that; maybe you stole his car to get him involved; maybe you killed that old woman hoping to pin it on him. Ridiculous, I know, but tell that to a man crazy-drunk."

Not so ridiculous. I was everybody's favorite suspect. Except Brennan's, oddly enough.

"What do you want me to do, Debbie? Do you want to stay here for a while?"

"No. I don't want to alarm Cindy—she's with Mother now. Pat's never bothered Cindy, or Mother, so I think the two of them'll be all right." She shivered.

"Where are you living?"

"We have an apartment downtown. Could you … would you stay with us tonight? I can tell Cindy you're a friend of the family or an uncle or something."

This was the dream of a lifetime, but I had hoped to start poking into things tonight, contacting a few people who I thought could help me uncover some things regarding Mrs. Jonsen's murder. But maybe this was worth the time at that. Maybe Pat Nelson *was* involved in the murder and was being either cute or stupid.

"Okay," I said. "Be glad to."

She leaned over, touched a hand to my face. "Mal."

"Yeah?"

"Can I do something I wanted to do for a long time?"

I shrugged. "Sure."

"Good," she said, and smiled her tiny smile.

And kissed me.

14

As old, remodeled apartments go, Debbie's wasn't so bad. It was located on Second Street, in the block where the downtown makes its last gasp and the slope of West Hill takes over. About a third of the places of business on her block had new brick fronts and had witnessed considerable self-initiated urban renewal by forward-looking landlords; but she had her run-down neighbors, too: several bars, a pair of sagging, empty warehouses, and the old union hall.

Below Debbie was a nice bar/restaurant owned by one of the conscientious landlords, who had seen to it that the apartment was freshly wallpapered and supplied with new kitchen appliances. The rest of her apartment, though, was clearly much as it had been, say, fifty years ago. The ceilings were high and of gray, faded plaster edged with plaster rococo—not unlike the wood carving at Mrs. Fox's, only the work of a far less talented craftsman. The floors were bare dark wood, the varnish mostly worn away. It had apparently come furnished, because a secondhand-store decor was mixed oddly with things Debbie and her husband had bought, like the twenty-five-inch TV and the stereo console in the living room.

After climbing up the narrow and gloomy stairwell, we entered into the daughter's room, with its pink wallpaper and fuzzy pink throw rugs, scattered like discarded old sweaters of

Debbie's. A door straight ahead led to the bleak, brown master bedroom; a doorless archway to the right led to the kitchen, and through the kitchen was the living room, with its light blue wallpaper smattered with dark blue flowers, soft-focus lighting coming from standing lamps. A pleasant enough, very much lived-in apartment.

An apartment a man had lived in. In the living room was a gun rack with three balsa-wood models of Winchester rifles, as well as two crossed swords on a tin shield, and over the bed were two pseudo-authentic dueling pistols on plaques—phallic symbols all, left behind (consciously or not) to remind anyone who entered this apartment that a man had been with the woman who slept here.

"Can I ask you something?" I said.

Debbie had decided to leave her daughter at her mother's for the night. We were sitting on a black imitation-leather couch in the living room, sipping glasses of Pepsi. Debbie didn't keep beer in the house. It was cold in there, an air conditioner chugging away in the bottom of a big bay window across the room. I was half-turned, studying a large frame behind the couch, a frame exhibiting half a dozen license plates; the two plates closest to my line of vision were number two from one year ago and number one from two years ago.

"What do you want to ask?" she said.

"Something about your husband."

"Let's hear it."

"Why in God's name does he go lusting after these damn license plates? What in hell possesses him?"

"What makes anyone go after something?" she said. "What makes anyone try to be first at anything?"

"But something so absurd, so pointless...." I stopped myself short. I was going condescending on her.

"I suppose I agree," she said, with her tiny smile, "but it's one of the more harmless things a man like Pat might decide to pursue. But I must say I don't enjoy camping out in the cold dead of winter on the courthouse lawn, teeth chattering all night, waiting to dash into the building next morning and fight and claw toward the license counter." She laughed. "Have to admit, though, that year we got license plate number one was kind of a thrill."

I shook my head, laughed, and said, "To each his own, I guess. You think Pat'll come around tonight and bother us?"

"Hard to say. Could be he won't show up at all. Could be he'll show sooner than tonight ... could be any time now. He's already roaring drunk."

"How can he get away with that, getting drunk on a Friday afternoon? Doesn't he have a job?"

"He used to work at Ribbed-Stone Silo, but he quit a few months ago and went to work for a friend of his who lets him keep loose hours. This friend, Chet Richards, runs a nursery."

"Your husband changes *diapers* for a living?"

She let out a giggle that took me back to junior high. "Plants and trees, not kids, silly. Anyway, it's a good job, in its way ... not particularly good-paying, as you can see by our surroundings ... but he's got lots of freedom, and besides, Pat really likes outdoor work."

"Can I ask some more questions, on the personal side?"

"You can ask whatever you want to, Mal, if you'll just stay here with me. I don't like the idea of having to face Pat when he's the way he is right now."

"Okay, then. When kind of marriage has it been, anyway? I mean you're not newlyweds; you've been married for what, at least twelve years? Cindy's eleven."

"Not quite that long." Her cheeks reddened a little. "Cindy came along pretty early that first year we were married, if you know what I mean."

I knew what she meant, and shouldn't have embarrassed her like that, but I'd completely forgotten that she had dropped out of school midway through her last semester as a senior, to marry Pat Nelson.

"It's been a good enough marriage," she said, still a bit flushed. "Pat's a quiet person, usually. Spends a lot of time doing male things ... hunting, poker with his buddies a couple times a week, sports on TV on the weekend ... but he loves little Cindy. He's been good to her, and treated me pretty well until this drinking thing started. Me, I've had my own friends to spend time with, and Cindy, and Mother."

"When did it go sour?" I said. "How long has this beating and drinking nonsense been going on?"

"Not long. Less than a year, I'd say. He didn't like his job at Ribbed-Stone—not anymore, anyway. See, there was a change in management; the son of the guy who founded the silo company took over when his dad retired. This son is a college-kid type: nice enough, but not Pat's idea of a boss. He was discontented because of that, started drinking a couple nights a week, and started beating on me along with it. I thought when he changed jobs he'd get back to normal. No such luck. Oh, he was happy in his new job, happier anyway, but his drinking pattern was set by then, and he kept right on with it. And ..." She touched my arm, moved closer on the couch. "... he thinks I've been cheating on him. He's very paranoid about it, as you can tell from this crazy idea he has about you and me having an affair."

"Is there ... any basis to his suspicions? After all, you did say he was out with the boys a lot."

She looked hurt for a moment, then said, "Of course not. I'm too busy for any stupid hanky-panky silliness. I have Cindy to raise, and I have my job.... Well, I used to have it, anyway."

"You lost your job?"

She nodded. "I was a secretary. Worked for William Morgan."

"The attorney?"

Another nod. "But when Pat started in on his drinking and all, I got less efficient and was let go. Haven't found anything since."

I could understand how she could lose her job; a legal secretary has to be perfection personified, and outside pressure of the sort her husband had exerted on Debbie would've been plenty to throw her off.

"I'll tell you something, Mal. I'll tell you something about how faithful I've been to that damn husband of mine. Not only was I faithful to him when he was going out with his stupid friends all the time, playing poker and hunting and that damn drinking; not only that, but you're the first, the very first man I've been alone with since Pat moved out of here.... Even now, even when I'm through with the bum, I've been faithful to him. Out of dumb habit, I guess. Isn't that silly?"

"Kind of," I said.

"I think it is," she said firmly. "Silly."

She was sitting very close now.

"Me too," I said. "Silly."

"Silly," she agreed.

The fuzzy pink sweater was soft and warm under my hands; it slipped off so easy, and I felt the soft coolness of her flesh. Her bra was one of those no-bra things and came off in a whisper; her breasts were large without sagging, her nipples small and as pink as her sweater. The skirt came off as easy as the bra, then the pantyhose and panties, and we kissed and fondled. My clothes gradually came off somehow or other, and soon I was nuzzling the full breasts of the girl I'd so longed to kiss in junior high, enjoying the slightly plump but nicely formed body of Debbie Lee, a small woman but with plenty of everything, proof positive that good things come in small packages, and we made love there, slowly, on the cool imitation leather of the couch, beneath the framed license plates.

15

When the heat of the moment subsided, the cold of the air conditioner took over. My exposed backside was invaded by goose pimples, and they spread to the rest of me and then to the cooling body beneath me. We jumped up and got into our clothes as quickly as we'd gotten out of them. The only pause in the procedure was as I was slipping my shirt on, when Debbie took a moment to caress my bruised side with gentle, sympathetic fingertips.

Dressed again, we sat shyly next to each other on the couch, and as the coldness of the air conditioning had pretty much nipped in the bud any afterplay, we began to kiss, tentatively, like high school kids out parking for the first time. We must've kissed for an hour, making up for all that lost time from our adolescence. We kissed till our lips were numb. Necked is what we did, but no heavy petting. For some ungodly reason, after our horny humping on black imitation leather, I found myself chastely restraining my roving hands, touching nary a breast, plumbing not a panty. You figure it out.

After a while we stroked each other's cheeks—a simultaneous, coincidental touching that made for a nice moment, giving a semblance of depth to our hastily thrown-together relationship. No talking had gone on for some time. We had nothing in particular to say to each other; this was just a renewal of that thing between us that had never gotten off the ground in previous years. There was a juvenile aspect to our coupling, our necking; we were a pair of would-be Wright Brothers who had given up the dream years ago and then come back in an age of jets with a terrific new glider.

We got up from the couch. Debbie straightened her clothes and poked at her hair, none of which affected the pleasantly tousled, just-been-had-and-liked-it look she had about her. I went to the big bay window and glanced out at darkness. We'd necked ourselves into evening. Considering how I had planned to get into my Sherlock Holmes number today, time had been wasted. But sex is never a waste of time, really. Or if it is, name some better way to waste it.

She asked what I wanted for supper, and I told her.

"Mal," she blushed, "don't be gross."

A teenager's word: gross. It was charming to hear her say that, somehow.

"All right, then," I said. "What have you got that's quick?"

"I make a mean plate of spaghetti. I have some French bread I got at the store this morning that'll go with it perfect."

"Good. Can I help?"

"What?"

"Can I help? Help you in the kitchen?"

"Are you kidding?"

"No, I'm not kidding. Why would I be kidding?"

"I don't know. It's just that Pat…."

"Pat never helped you in the kitchen."

"Nope," she admitted, with a little grin. "Woman's work. He's never offered to help once."

"Well then," I said, rolling up imaginary sleeves, "let's go into that kitchen and strike a blow for Women's Lib."

"Okay," she said. "Let's."

I made the spaghetti. The noodle part, I mean. Got some water boiling in a big kettle and added some vegetable oil, just a drop, to keep the strands from sticking together, and stood and stirred and preened over the thing. Meanwhile Debbie was making a homemade sauce with an aroma an Italian would die for (or, if he was in the Mafia, kill for). She also took care of wrapping up the French bread in foil and shoving it in the oven.

Again, we didn't say much as we made the meal, but we had a good time, bustling around together in the kitchen, in mutual effort. The meal was as enjoyable, and as silent, as its preparation. Debbie dimmed the lights in the kitchen, obscuring the contrast of shiny new appliances and ancient wall of cabinets, plopped a fat red candle down center-table, and lit it, sending a soft glow of light around the table as we ate. The candle was scented—strawberry, I think—it added much to the romantic atmosphere. All we lacked was some damn fool playing a violin.

After the wordless, candlelit dinner, Debbie shattered the mood with a flick of a light switch, and we were back in a kitchen again. I helped her clear the table (getting a raised eyebrow of wonderment) and went to the sink and got a sinkful of soapy suds going.

"What are you doing?" she asked.

"I'm washing the dishes. You dry."

"I don't believe it."

"No big chivalrous deal. I'm just used to a bachelor existence, in which I have to do my own chores anyway. I can't afford a live-in maid."

She joined me at the sink, got a towel from somewhere, and I handed her the dishes one by one as I cleaned them. "Well," she said, "it's a pleasant change from Pat. He likes me in the kitchen or in bed, and that's about it."

I shrugged. "I might be the same way if I were a married man. It's pretty well instilled in our culture, don't you think? We see our parents behaving in a pattern and we just fall into it ourselves after a time."

"Even when we don't like it?"

"Sure. Because it's all we know."

"I suppose you're right. Mal?"

"Yeah?"

"What would it have been like?"

"What would what have been like?"

"Us. You and me. If we had gotten together instead of Pat and me."

"I don't know. Different than you and Pat, sure. But not like it would be now."

"What do you mean?"

"Well, if I'd married you straight out of high school, I'd be a different person than I am right now."

"You mean if you hadn't bummed around like you did for those years."

"I take some issue with the term 'bummed,' my dear. I worked. Did a little of everything. Construction and cop, and a reporter for a while…. That was the best, I suppose, that last one. Bummed is not the word. Bummer might be, for the short time I was involved in the Haight-Ashbury scene."

"How heavy were you into that? Drugs, I mean."

"Not very heavy. Got scared out before much happened … to me, anyway. Was doing grass, which is no big thing, and was just into speed when, fortunately for me but unfortunately for him, this friend of mine overdosed on the stuff." I shuddered at the involuntary image that flashed through my mind: my buddy Chuck, floating dead in his bathtub, his eyes two big, lifeless marbles, hair like so much dead seaweed. "It was a long time ago," I said. I gave her a look that said I didn't want to talk about that subject any longer.

But she pursued it just the same, in an oblique way, asking, "What made you do all that?"

"All what?"

"All of it ... all those different jobs, and then the drugs...."

"I don't know. I suppose it was just getting out of the service, after goddamn Vietnam. Coming home and having my folks die. Had nobody here in Port City, really—no relatives; most of my friends were moved away or married; I couldn't see sticking around. So I took off and searched around, trying to find some way to make life ... *mean* something, I guess. Same reason for the drug bit, too; some kind of half-ass search for meaning, for identity."

She thought about that a second, then said, "Mal?"

"Yeah?"

"You think you'll find it back here? In Port City?"

"No. I quit looking."

"What do you mean?"

"I mean I decided to quit wasting my time looking for the Holy Grail. There ain't none. I decided to accept my lot in life as just another dumb animal who won't ever understand a goddamn thing."

"How come you never got married?"

"Don't know. Maybe I'm gay."

She smiled and said, "I don't think you'd have much luck convincing me of that."

"Well, maybe I just haven't met the right girl yet. Maybe I never really got over you, Debbie."

"Don't be silly! Besides, I've heard about you."

"Heard what about me?"

"I got an aunt that lives over by you."

"Oh?"

"And she's told me about you. She'll say, 'You know what your old boyfriend's up to now?' And then she tells me. I know you sold a mystery book, too. I saw the article in the paper."

"I didn't know you'd stayed that interested in me."

"Who says I was, silly. Maybe I just have a busybody aunt who likes to gossip."

"Are you talking about Thelma Parker? Is she your aunt?"

"Yes."

"Well, you do have a busybody aunt at that. Ole Thelma Parker spends half her waking hours giving me the evil eye."

Debbie giggled. "She even has binoculars."

"No kidding?"   ·

"She told me you were seeing a girl who worked at the hospital. What was she, a nurse or something?"

"Nope. Dietician out there. She's the one you can thank for my being so well trained into doing the dishes and such. A real liberated female, that one."

"I'm jealous."

"Jealous? Christ, girl, you're the one who's married! I'm a poor bachelor who gets it on maybe a dozen times a year if he's lucky, and you're a mother and the veteran of a well-worn marriage bed to boot. It's not like you been sitting around in a chastity belt for the last ten years, waiting for me to come home from the Crusades."

She laughed and took the last of the dishes from me, wiped it off, and stacked it with the rest on the counter. "I'll put 'em away later," she said, and led me into the living room, back to the couch.

"I'm sorry, Mal," she said, twining her fingers in my hair. "I can't help being nosy about you. Can't help wondering what you been up to all this time. And I can't help wondering what it would've been like if things had worked out ... different ... with you and me."

The shrill sound of the phone ringing out in the kitchen cut into our conversation.

Debbie rose to answer it, saying, "Be right back," and headed out there.

I could hear her muffled voice, but couldn't make out the words. She came back a few moments later, visibly shaken.

"It's Pat," she said.

"Yeah? Where was he calling from?"

"Downstairs. There's a pay phone in the bar downstairs."

"What did he say?"

"He said he knows you're up here with me."

This time he was right, wasn't he? We had confirmed his suspicions; paranoia, as usual, was a self-fulfilling prophecy.

"Does he have a key?" I asked.

"No. I had the locks changed after he left."

"Then to hell with him. We won't let him in."

"He says he wants you to come down there and ... fight him like a man."

"Oh, for Christ's sake."

"He says if you don't, he'll come up here and break the door down. He ... he has a knife."

Pat hadn't changed much over the years, had he? He was still sending people around telling me about him and his knife.

"What's he going to do?" I asked. "Stab down the door? I say the hell with him. Forget about him."

"No. No, that's not the way to handle him. I'm going down and talk to him. Maybe he'll listen to reason."

"Oh Christ, Debbie, get serious...."

"Let me try."

"Debbie."

"Please."

"Okay. He's your husband. Do it however you want."

"Thanks, Mal."

"For what?"

I followed her through the bedroom into Cindy's room. I stood beside the squat brown heater and watched her open the door and disappear from sight, going down the stairs. Her footsteps made slow, steady clops.

I waited. Listened.

I heard Debbie's muffled voice, but I couldn't make out the words.

And then a sound I could make out: the sharp sound of a slap. And another recognizable sound followed right after: that of feet scurrying up the stairs, panic-driven feet.

Debbie slammed the door and looked at me, her face crimson on the left side from the slap, and said, "He's so drunk he's crazy. He says ... he says come down and fight him like a man, or he'll come up here and ... and cut you."

Well.

Looked like Pat Nelson and I were going to have our showdown at last. High Noon had taken over a decade to get here, but here it was.

I walked to the door and opened it. Descended the stairs, the walls claustrophobically tight on me. Down at the bottom, in a pool of dim light from a twenty-five-watt bulb next to the tenant mailboxes, was Pat Nelson. I could smell the booze immediately, growing noticeably stronger as I neared him.

He was a mess. He was wearing a tee-shirt with booze soaked down the front of it; his blue jeans, too, were wet with liquor. He was tall, thin to the point of undernourishment, his cheeks still spotted with hints of acne; his hair was right out of the fifties: dyed blond greaser's hair, with long dark skinny sideburns. His eyes drooped and his lower lip protruded, as if James Dean were the latest thing. His nose was pug, the sort a teenaged girl might find cute—which was his whole problem, really; he was somebody who'd been "cute" ten years ago and had tried to retain the image. He was what the phrase "callow youth" is all about, only he wasn't a youth.

"Mallory," he slurred, a near parody of a drunk, "you goddamn bastard, Mallory, put up your hands and fight like a man."

I punched him once, right in his pug nose, and he went down like an armful of kindling wood.

I headed back up the stairs.

Behind me he was pulling himself back together, pulling himself back onto his feet like the Frankenstein monster coming to life for the first time.

"Mallory!" he shouted, and his voice echoed in the stairwell like somebody shouting down a crap hole. "Mallory, you goddamn bastard, what are you doing with my wife in there!"

And he scrambled up the steps, which I'd climbed about halfway, and I turned my head and saw the glint of his knife in his hand. When I turned, he froze, down two steps from me, and held the knife up for me to see and be scared of.

But it was just a little thing—shiny, probably razor sharp, but a real anticlimax, not much bigger than a pen knife. Oh, it could kill you, but I couldn't see getting upset about it.

I was just high enough above him to be able to kick the thing out of his hand, and it went clumpety-clump down a couple of steps and lay there. Then I gave him a hard forearm across the chest, and he went clumpety-clump down all the steps and lay there. It wasn't far enough a fall to hurt him bad, and he was too drunk to feel it, and after he'd looked up at me drunkenly for a moment, he went to sleep.

I walked to the top of the stairs, where I found Debbie standing in the doorway, her face ashen. But she said nothing.

We spent a quiet evening listening to old records that had been popular when we were in school, and when we talked, it wasn't about Pat, but about old times and old friends, and sometimes about her daughter Cindy. We slept on the couch under a light blanket that protected us from the chugging air conditioner; it was cramped there on the couch, but Debbie was small and we made a nice fit, and neither one of us felt like sleeping in their bed—Pat's and hers—though it never came up in conversation.

16

It wasn't a good day for a funeral.

The morning sky was as clear and blue as the surface of a quiet lake. The sun was a cheerful yellow ball. A cooling breeze rolled in off the trees surrounding the cemetery. In those same trees, birds were chirping pleasantly, almost disrespectfully. By all rights it should've been miserable. Overcast. Maybe raining. But it wasn't. It was beautiful. Not a good day for a funeral at all.

Which was okay, because Edward Jonsen had decided against it, anyway. Having a funeral for his mother, that is. He'd had no crystal ball to predict this nonfunereal day; he had just decided to spare all expense.

So there had been no funeral. The paper last night had said, "Graveside services" in lieu of anything else, and here I now was, watching Mrs. Jonsen get planted in the earth, a cold seed not expected to grow. The final resting place for Edward Jonsen's mother was the family plot, next to her long-gone husband Elwood; her half of the stone had been inscribed years ago, with only the death date freshly chiseled in, unweathered. The casket was a black metallic thing, hardly lavish, but at least it wasn't a pine box. The service consisted of three minutes of mumbling from some clergyman acquaintance of Jonsen's.

There were, however, lots of flowers crowded around the graveside, and lots of friends, too: over twenty of them huddled

97

around the hole, looking irritated at the son's lack of respect for his mother and her death. Most were elderly, peers of Mrs. Jonsen who had made a real effort to come out here, suffering the inconvenience out of a desire to say good-bye to a friend.

Next to Jonsen was an attractive woman of about forty who resembled Mrs. Jonsen a great deal. I took her to be Jonsen's sister. She was a dark-eyed brunette and was dressed in black, of course, but with no hat and veil, and looked vaguely irritated herself. Whether with Edward Jonsen or just who, I didn't know.

I was soon to find out.

Directly after the mumble-mouth minister dismissed the disgruntled flock, she approached me. "Are you Mr. Mallory?"

"I'm Mallory, yes," I said, apprehensive. After all, her brother had pulled a gun on me just the day before.

"I'm Ann Bloom. Ann Jonsen Bloom. Edward is my brother, and…." She glanced over at the open grave. "… that sweet woman was my mother. Could I have a word with you?"

"Sure."

We walked over to a clump of trees. Edward, in a tentlike gray suit, was standing alone by the graveside. Only one or two people had stopped to speak a word of consolation to him; the others were evidently bitter about what they considered to be his hasty and thoughtless farewell to his mother. Now he was staring at us, his sister and me, clenching and unclenching his fists, obviously wishing he could hear our conversation, and also obviously resenting that conversation.

Ann Jonsen Bloom said, "Forgive my brother. He's the product of too much pampering … the self-centered baby of our family. One of these moments he'll realize he's lost the only person in the world who cared about him, and it'll hurt him.

Right now all that is on his mind is the money he's lost because of the robbery."

She paused and gave me a chance to say something, but I had nothing to say. She said, "Edward's prime concern is money. He's had dreams for years of Mother's hidden fortune falling into his hands, and with some justification; he knew that he was the sole heir of her will."

"Why is that?"

"I'm left out of it at my own request, actually, because I knew Mother wanted to leave the bulk of her estate to Edward. You see, Mr. Mallory, I am married to a very wealthy man, and mother wanted to see that her money and valuables went to the one of her children who needed it most, and all I asked Mother for, when she was writing her will some years ago, was an oil portrait of her that was painted when she was in her twenties. And she gave that to me, then, on the spot."

"What about all those beautiful antiques of your mother's?"

"I have no interest in them, no use for them, no room for them. We live in a two-hundred-year-old house filled with the relics of my husband's family ... the possessions of several generations of wealth ... and I've come to detest the sight of an antique. We spend our happiest time, my family, in a relatively simple summer cottage in the Ozarks. Possessions are a bother. The only thing of my mother's I want to keep is her memory. I want to hold the memory of her close to me for the rest of my life. Edward can have the rest. The money. The things."

"If they're found."

"If they're found," she nodded. "I'm ... I'm so embarrassed by this poor excuse for a service. I called Edward last night, and he said he'd made the arrangements, and when I got here this morning—flew in from Philadelphia; that's where we live, where my husband and my two boys and I live—when I got here this morning, this shabby little graveside affair is all Edward had arranged. He was … excuse me for being frank, but … he was just too damn cheap to arrange anything better."

"Well," I said, "it won't matter to your mother. The funeral racket is pretty lousy anyway. I don't blame anybody for resisting that stupid an expense."

She said, "Thanks for trying to make me feel better, but it won't do any good. I was raised traditionally, raised to believe in ceremony and respect, and so was Edward. Mother would have wanted a nice service, a church service. She even had a program written out for the service as she wanted it: the songs she wanted sung, a eulogy for old Clancy Rogers to read, the retired Methodist minister who married Sam and me…." Something caught in her throat; her face reddened. She dug into her purse, found a Kleenex, dabbed her eyes, and blew her nose.

"I … I want to thank you for being nice to Mother. She wrote about you in her last letter. About what a nice young man you were, and how she enjoyed talking to you. And … and let me say that I think it was very sweet of you to come today."

"It's nothing."

"It's a lot. You care more about her death than that fat, spoiled son of hers." Her face reddened again, this time with rage. "I … I want to apologize for what … what Edward did yesterday. He told me about it—I don't know what the *real* story is; probably even more embarrassing than the one Edward told me. He told me he confronted you with this idea of his that you … stole…." She stopped, let out a feeble smile, and shook her head.

"Listen," I said, "it's okay. He's bound to be upset."

"Upset! He's a damn fool. Excuse my frankness. I talked to Sheriff Brennan about you, and he told me how utterly ridiculous Edward's suspicions are, and he told me how extremely hurt you were by my mother's death." She managed another, less feeble smile. "And not just the physical injury those toughs gave you—not just the physical abuse, and the abuse my brother gave you yesterday. But that you were moved by her death. That you cared. Thank you for that, Mr. Mallory. And I'll do my best to see my brother doesn't interfere with your life again."

I smiled back at her. "You know something, Mrs. Bloom?"

"What?"

"You remind me of your mother. And that's the nicest compliment I can think of to pay you."

Her eyes clouded up, but she was still smiling. Quickly, she kissed my cheek, then turned and walked over and joined her brother.

I headed back to the grassy parking area inside the cemetery gate, trying not to trip over too many of the stone reminders of the people underfoot. Only one person of those who had attended the service was still around: Sheriff Brennan. He had stood directly across the grave from me during the would-be preacher's slipshod hocus-pocus, and now he was leaning against his official car (or "unit," as we ex-cops call it), and he seemed to be waiting to talk to me.

"Howdy, Brennan."

"Mallory," he nodded.

"What were you doing here today?"

"Same thing as you."

"Oh?"

"Watching faces. Checking reactions out."

I grinned. "Come up with any conclusions?"

"Nope. An opinion, though."

"Let's hear it."

"Edward Jonsen is a horse's ass."

"Agreed. But his sister is a fine lady."

"Agreed. A fine lady. Spoke to her this morning."

"So I gathered. Sounds like you even said some nice things about me. What's the matter, Brennan? You slipping?"

"Maybe. Just pay attention to what I have to say next."

"Which is?"

"Nothing you haven't heard before. Just that I don't want you nosing into this."

"I haven't been." And that was true, really. Hadn't done anything much yet. Oh, I'd been beat up twice and threatened with guns and knives. But nothing active.

"What were you doing here, then, Mallory?"

"We already went over that."

"That's right. And you admitted you were here to study the people, see their reactions, which means you're nosing around."

"Did I admit that?"

"I believe so."

"I don't remember admitting that. Brennan?"

"Yeah?"

"Have you cracked the case yet?"

"Sure. That's why I'm standing here telling you to lay off it."

"Well what *have* you come up with?"

"The only thing I got to tell you is this: stay home like a good boy. Okay?"

"Oh, sure. So what have you come up with so far?"

Brennan sighed. "Not much, to be truthful. I thought we had something; we tied three of the break-ins to a travel agency.

I mean, three of the families were on vacation when their homes were broke into, and all three had the same travel agency."

"But then Port City only *has* one travel agency."

"Right. So I end up with a handful of air. If the travel agency is the source of their information, why would it turn up only three times?"

"Maybe they've got more than one source."

"Maybe. If they were pros, I'd think so. But these people are amateurs—look at that poor old lady dying. An accident. The kind a pro would avoid." He grunted. "Like I said, any time you want to swap theories, look me up. But otherwise, keep your damn nose out. Understood?"

"Understood."

He glanced out across the cemetery toward where Mrs. Jonsen was resting. His son John was buried here, too. "Hell of a thing," he said. His jaw got firm, and he climbed in his car and pulled away.

I stood and thought for five minutes or so, then did the same.

17

After the nine-thirty service for Mrs. Jonsen, I headed straight back to Debbie's and got there by ten-thirty for a late breakfast. Debbie hadn't wanted me to leave, still fearing what Pat might pull, and on my return I found that she had surrounded herself with company (or protection); daughter Cindy was back from her overnight stay with Debbie's mother, and a friend of Debbie's was there, too: a busty frosted blonde of about thirty in a sheer white blouse and dark blue ski pants. She was a good-looking woman, but wore rather severe makeup that gave her a hard look. Teeth stained from tobacco further took the edge off her mostly attractive appearance. Her name was Sarah Petersen, and she and her husband "ran a business." She didn't have much to say to me beyond that.

Something was in the air, and I couldn't tell what. Tension of some sort. Sarah had a sour expression, and even the cute Cindy, looking like Debbie must've at eleven, seemed ill at ease. I began to sense I'd come in on the middle of something. An argument, probably.

Everybody else had already eaten their breakfast, but Debbie had kept some rolls warming in the oven for me and proceeded to scramble a couple eggs for me while I sat at the table and made a few vain attempts to engage Sarah in conversation. She wasn't buying. Like Debbie, Sarah wasn't exactly a chatterbox, but it was more than that, and I began to feel certain both women were mutually ticked off. As Debbie handed me the plate of scrambled eggs and breakfast fast rolls, Sarah rose suddenly and stalked out of the apartment.

"What's with her?" I asked Debbie.

"Cindy," Debbie said, "go to the living room, will you? Go in the living room and read your book."

"Can I watch TV instead, Mommy?" The little girl's eyes were as blue and saucerlike as her mother's. She was a tiny thing and looked good in the lacy pink little dress she was wearing.

"Of course you can watch TV, honey. Go on now. Scoot."

The child didn't back-talk her mother. She got up from the table like a little lady, giving me a quick, big grin that told me she was eager to get acquainted. The tension of the scene when I'd arrived had evidently stifled the child's natural curiosity about this stranger her mother had introduced as "Mr. Mallory, a friend," and she would have plenty of questions for me later. She bounced out.

"Sweet-looking little kid," I said.

"Yes, she is," Debbie said, coming out of her uneasy mood with a smile of pride. "Thank God Pat hasn't taken to beating *her.*"

"Hey, listen, I repeat: what's with that Petersen woman?"

"We were in the midst of an argument when you came in, or did you gather that?"

"I gathered. What caused the tiff?"

"Well, it's my fault, really. I shouldn't have called her to come over, should've had better sense. She and her husband are ... were? ... good friends of Pat and me, and I thought Sarah would stand behind me in this unpleasant situation. Up till now she's seemed sympathetic, but come to think of it, ever since the trouble started, she's encouraged me to try to patch things up with Pat."

"Meaning she wasn't happy to hear you had an overnight guest last night."

"She sure wasn't. And evidently Pat went over there last night, after he'd sobered up—or healed up, or whatever—and told them quite a different story. About how my new boyfriend attacked him."

I shook my head, smiling humorlessly. "She *was* a bad choice to have come over."

"Couldn't have been worse. Here I was asking her for protection because I didn't feel secure here alone, didn't know what Pat would do after last night, and she comes over and gives me a sermon about what a bad wife I am. I mean—"

"Yeah. I know what you mean. What about Cindy?"

"She was in reading her book and didn't hear any of it, or much of it anyway, thank God. When Cindy came in for breakfast, just a few minutes before you showed up, the argument continued, but in an understated way that I don't think Cindy could pick up on."

"I don't know. Kids are pretty hip. Eleven years old isn't babe-in-arms, you know."

She nodded. "Yes, Cindy realizes things are pretty rocky with her father and me; I can't hope to hide that from her. But I *can* protect her from some of it. From stupid, catty bitches like Sarah, I can protect her."

"And from knowing her mommy's shacking up with another guy."

"That, too." She let me see that tiny grin of hers, the one I fell in love with at thirteen. "Has it gone that far? Are we 'shacked up' now?"

I shrugged. "We'll see. We'll see what develops. We'll see what you decide to do about Pat."

"You mean … you think I ought to be talking to a lawyer. Think I ought to file the papers."

"It's your marriage. I'm glad to help you and delighted to … enjoy your company, let's say. But it's your marriage, your child, your life, your decision."

"You're right, Mal. But I'm not sure if … if I'm strong enough. In some ways I'm as much of a little girl as my daughter in there."

"Well, there's no time limit on it."

"On what?"

"Growing up."

She thought about that, started to say something, then decided against it. She rose and got me some coffee.

After a third cup (she made great coffee, that woman; her years with Pat had honed her kitchen abilities to a fine edge), I got up from the table, kissed her cheek in thanks, and said, "Can I use your phone?"

"Sure."

"You mind if I revert to chauvinist and let you do the dishes by yourself this time?"

"Not at all. I'm used to it. Go ahead, make your call."

I went to the phone on the wall and looked up George Price's number in the book.

George Price was a black guy who lived a few blocks from me on East Hill. A huge man who was beefy but not fat, George was around fifty years old but could have passed for thirty-five, easy. His face was broad, dominated by a big, disarming, dazzling white grin that had (added to some hard work and perseverance) made George many a dollar over the years. George owned the whole block he lived on and had built (with the help of various of his six sons) his own home and rebuilt most of the other houses on that block. He was, as he put it, "a blackjack of all trades" and liked to refer to himself as "the poor man." How many poor men do you know that own their whole block?

George was a plumber. And a TV repairman. And a farmer for hire. Also an auto mechanic. Anything, in fact, that could be broken George could fix. He was one of those guys who buys something and, before using it, takes the thing apart to make sure he knows how it ticks, in case a breakdown should occur.

He was also a bit of a con man, as his "poor man" routine might indicate. He could bullshit his way right into your heart, and your pocketbook, but he was very good about standing behind whatever it was he sold you, and generally fixed up whatever it was you bought from him even after his generous personal warranty had run out. For $250 I'd bought a color TV from George just last year, a like-new set that, as George put it, had "a picture more natural than my natural."

Because he was black, and because he sold things cheap, many of his Port City customers assumed George's merchandise was obtained in some less-than-legal way. I didn't believe that, but since so many people did, I thought George would be a good bet for some information.

"How you doin', Mallory? That TV set hasn't conked out on you, has it? If it has, the poor man'll fix it up for you. That's how I keep my customers happy, you know; a poor man has to treat his friends right."

I could picture his wide grin as I heard the deep bass voice roll out over the phone. I let him continue with his good-natured bullshit for a while, then cut in.

"George," I said, "There's nothing wrong with my set. It's beautiful."

"You need something else, then? How 'bout a videotape machine? You ain't in control of your life if you ain't in control of your TV, you know."

"George."

"Yeah, Mallory?"

"I'm not buying anything, George."

"Not buyin' anything?"

"No, George."

"What, then?"

"I need some help."

"That toilet of yours backin' up again? We can get that took care of in a flush."

"George, not that kind of help. Information."

"Information?"

"Yeah. You know those break-ins that've been going on lately?"

"Sure do. Got my gun by my bed. Look after that whole damn block of mine. No no-good freeloader's going to lift any of my stuff. What's wrong with people? Don't they know you got to work for what you get? Nothin' comes free."

"It does for these guys. There's been eight break-ins so far, and an old lady got killed in the process of the last one."

"Yeah, I heard about that. Shame. Say, weren't you the guy that found the old gal's body?"

"That's right."

"And now you want to find these guys yourself?"

"That's right, George, and before you try to sell me a gun, let me ask you something. Can you tell me the names of anybody in town who might be peddling hot merchandise?"

"Mallory, you know me better than that. Don't hurt the poor man's pride. You know my prices are low 'cause I buy from people direct and I got low overhead, and—"

"George. I don't think you're involved with these rip-off guys. But lots of people would assume that you *do* deal in hot goods because you sell stuff right out of your house, your prices are low, and…." I hesitated.

"And 'cause I'm black. Yeah, I suppose you're right. But so what? So what if people think that? I'm not into hot goods, and that's that."

"I just thought that, since some people do assume you handle that sort of merchandise, maybe somebody's approached you about selling their stolen goods."

"Using me as a fence, you mean?"

"Yeah."

"Well. I don't know, Mallory."

"George, it's important. So far these guys have stolen God knows how much, killed one lady, and beat the hell out of me twice."

"And you're still messin' with them? You feelin' all right?"

"No, I'm not. I won't feel all right until these SOBs are put away where they can't hurt anybody or steal anything again."

"I don't go for guys like that myself. People got to work for what they get."

"I agree, George. Can you help me?"

"This is strict between us, right?"

"Strict between us."

"There's a place in South End. A used auto parts shop on one side, a big old empty garage on the other. Place is called Tony's."

"Living quarters above?"

"Yeah. It's all one big double-story building, living quarters on top, garage and auto parts deal below. Ratty-lookin' place. You know it?"

"I know it."

"I hear—just hear, now—you can get whatever you need from a guy there. A guy named P. J. somethin'."

"George, you're a prince."

"I'm just a poor man, Mallory, that's all."

"How can I thank you?"

"Forget it. But if you want to take a look at that videotape, we can swing you a deal."

"I'll think about it, George. Thanks again. See you."

"You be good now, Mallory. And more important ... be careful."

We hung up.

Debbie was just finishing up the dishes. I joined her, took the towel from her, and dried the last few.

"What's going on, Mal?" she said, nodding toward the phone on the wall.

"Nothing."

"Are you into something dangerous?"

"No."

"Aren't you going to stay here with me today?"

"I'm going to take care of some errands this afternoon. I'll be back this evening."

"Won't you please stay? I'm ... I'm still scared of what Pat might do."

"Keep the door locked and bolted. You'll be okay. If you aren't, call Lou Brown and he'll help you out."

"Lou Brown? Isn't he the deputy sheriff?"

"He's one of 'em. But he's a friend and'll keep it quiet, and nonofficial. Okay?"

"Come back as soon as you can?"

"I promise."

"I'll fix a nice supper for you."

"Really? What are we having?"

She dried her hands and put them around my neck and kissed me, then looked at me and said, "Anything you want."

"What time do you want me back?" I said.

18

Port City doesn't have a slum. What it does have, here and there, is "substandard housing," the largest concentration of which is located in that area of town known as South End. The word "slum" just isn't in the Port City vocabulary. To understand that you must keep in mind that Port City is Middle America, U.S.A., where the corn grows tall, grass is something you walk on, and everybody but me votes straight Republican; pleasantly dull ("A nice place to live, but you wouldn't want to visit there") and relentlessly middle-class. Even the millionaires like to think of themselves as middle-class joes. So do the slum dwellers.

And they have a point. If you tried to pass South End off as a slum to somebody born and bred in a big-city ghetto, you'd get laughed at or punched out. Because South End is, basically, a lower-middle-class residential district, having in common with East Hill a tendency toward conglomeration of different types of houses: everything from tumbledown shacks to brand-new pre-fabs. But the common denominator of South End housing is the one-story, rather run-down clapboard—in short, substandard. And so the bottom line comes to this: South End may not be a slum, but you'll sure bump into one hell of a lot of substandard housing down there.

Something else you'll bump into is industry. A good share of major local industry is situated in South End, the dominant one being the grain-processing plant, whose seasonal emissions of soybean fumes can turn a summer breeze into something you wouldn't care for. Another factory, where pumps of all sorts are manufactured, stands at the foot of West Hill bluff and marks the beginning of the End; a street cutting past the pump plant runs straight through the End and out of town, turning into Highway 61 South after a lengthy stretch littered with gas stations, used-car lots, hamburger palaces, and supermarkets, with the drab residential sections of South End cowering back behind all the plastic glitter. Just before the street turns officially into a highway, heading out to drive-in restaurants, motels, and melon stands, there is a big, many-laned intersection, and if you can maneuver your way into the left lane and turn, jostling across the railroad tracks, you'll find yourself in the heart of South End, staring smack at the huge grain-processing complex on the left hand and at Port City's literal wrong-side-of-the-tracks on the right. Just three blocks over those tracks was Tony's Used Auto Parts.

Across from Tony's, little raggedy kids were playing on the swings and slides in a large, well-tended park: two blocks' worth of land donated by the grain-processing people to the city to make up for smelling it up. One block of the park is taken up by a Little League baseball field with a stand of bleachers, in back of which is a graveled parking lot. That's where I left the van before crossing over to Tony's.

Tony's was an odd-looking, off-balance sort of a building; actually, it was two buildings slapped together: a tall, one-story garage fastened haphazardly to an equally tall but two-story arrangement of shop below, living quarters above. Together the joined buildings made for a big, long, sagging wooden ramshackle, with white-paint-faded-to-gray peeling to reveal even grayer wood. But the strangest-looking thing about this strange-looking structure was the windows; every window in the place was painted out with flat black. It didn't take Nero Wolfe to figure out the windows were black to keep people from seeing in.

Even the front shop-window was painted black. Nonprofessionally rendered lettering in white walked awkwardly across the black window, saying "Tony's Used Auto Parts," and in smaller, just-as-awkward letters: "If we don't have it, you don't need it." Okay.

I tried the shop's front door. Locked. They hadn't even bothered with a "Closed" sign. I walked around back of the building and found a rickety open stairway leading up to the back-door porch of the second-story living quarters. I climbed the stairs and knocked.

Nothing.

I knocked some more. Insistently.

The door cracked open, and one eye looked hesitantly out at me, like it was still Prohibition and the bathtub was full of gin. I repressed the urge to say Joe had sent me and said, "Is P. J. around?"

"Who wants him?" the eye said. It was a female voice and, as I studied it, a female eye, too. But from the sliver of pale face I could see along with the eye, I couldn't tell much else about who the eye and voice belonged to.

I said, "I heard P. J. sells stuff."

"He don't sell stuff anymore."

"But I heard…."

"I don't give a damn what you heard. He don't sell stuff anymore, and anyway, he don't never sell stuff to people he don't know, so get your goddamn ass off my porch."

"Please—"

And, delicate little thing that she was, she slammed the door on me.

I knocked again, and kept knocking, having decided I would go on knocking until I got some kind of response.

This time when the door opened, it was all the way. I didn't get much of a look inside the place, though, because something was blocking the view. What was blocking the view was a guy about the size of the Statue of Liberty's brother.

I said, "I, uh, I, uh…."

"You get outa here."

The voice was wrong, too high-pitched, but it didn't make him any less frightening. He was a square-jawed guy with a blond crew cut and dark eyes crowding a several-times-broken nose.

I said, "I, uh…."

"You're going down these steps. You get to choose how."

He gestured over the railing of the porch, pointing a finger that was like a section of lead pipe.

I chose.

I walked down the stairs, waving a little good-bye to the hulking figure in the doorway, and suddenly realized who he was. Or who he damn well might be.

That same hulking figure in the green van.

The one I had encountered at Mrs. Jonsen's that night, when I was trying to get license-plate numbers and instead ran into a glandular case loading up the van, who then ran into me and initiated all that Mallory-kicking.

Yes, he was the one. I was sure of it.

So I pretended to go away. I cut through the adjoining yard and headed down the street, which was a narrow lane lined with shade trees. I walked several blocks before ducking behind one of those trees to rest, think, hide. I'd gone in the opposite direction from where I'd left my van, simply because if Hulk and his honey were watching my exit, I didn't want to tip them as to where my car was. They hadn't seen me arrive (I hoped) and would assume I'd left my buggy down here somewhere, assume I'd gone to retrieve it and go.

It was a quiet street. No traffic. The warm afternoon sun was filtered and cooled through the shimmering leaves. The homes along the street were modest, standard South-End one-story clapboards, but well kept-up. A pleasant little neighborhood. High wild grass was growing up around the base of the tree where I was sitting, and I plucked a stalk and chewed the sweet root. I didn't mind sitting in the soothing shade of the tree, regrouping, waiting to see if Hulk or anybody followed me, waiting for five minutes to go by if he didn't.

When the five minutes had gone, I got up. Headed back to Tony's Used Auto Parts, circling around several blocks to waste some more time, and also in order to come up behind the building on the garage side. One nice thing about black-painted windows; just as I couldn't see in, they couldn't see out, and my approach was, I felt sure, undetected.

Next door to the garage was a run-down two-story gothic that was so close to its neighbor there was little more than a crawl space between them; it was a tight squeeze, but I had breathing room, and thanks to some bushes gone out-of-hand up by the gothic's porch, my presence wasn't likely to be noticed by passersby—out front, anyway. From the back I was pretty well exposed, though the passageway was dark enough to shelter me some.

I began examining the windows along the side of the garage. There were three of them, evenly spaced, and on the middle one I found a spot in the lower corner where some of its black paint had worn away a bit, or had maybe been scratched off. Heart pumping, I peeked in and saw nothing but the green of a vehicle of some kind.

Green?

I kept peeking, trying to tell whether or not that green vehicle was the same green vehicle I thought it was—namely, the green van that had been used to haul loot away from Mrs. Jonsen's.

I couldn't be sure.

There just wasn't enough of a peephole in the blackened window; not enough paint had been scraped or worn away. No way to tell for certain.

Except to get inside the garage and see for myself.

The street out in front of Tony's was well traveled, since it passed the grain-processing plant with its many employees, and also because it was one of the main entries to this South End residential section. But it was mid-afternoon, an off time, and the darkness of the space between garage and gothic, as well as those bushes blocking the way, made it hard (not impossible, but hard) for anyone going by in a car to see what I was going to do.

And what I was going to do was break the window.

Now wait a minute. I didn't go off half-cocked. I went off fully cocked. I first plastered my ear against the glass to check for any activity that might be going on in the garage. Not a sound. Then I very carefully slipped out of my short-sleeve sweatshirt and folded it, laid it gently against a pane of black-painted glass, and rammed my elbow into it.

The glass cracked.

It didn't shatter and go clattering to the floor, waking the dead and scaring hell out of the living; it just cracked, so that when I took the folded sweatshirt away, the framing wood still held the glass, slivered now in the formation of an interesting but simple jigsaw puzzle, and all that remained was to carefully, piece by piece, take apart that jigsaw puzzle, and then where a pane of glass had been would be a hole. I shook the loose glass from the sweatshirt, got back into it, and started picking the shards of glass from the window frame.

When I was done, I had a hole through which I could see the green vehicle completely. It was indeed a green van, but if it was the *same* green van, some changes had been made. For one thing, there were license plates, or one anyway; I had a back-angle view of the truck and could see a license plate where the van at Jonsen's had had none. Not that it was any great trick to take off or put on a plate, but it was a difference. A bigger difference was the red lettering on the side—GARDENING SERVICE—big, bold letters that hadn't been on the van I'd seen. Either the letters had been added since, or that night they'd been covered up somehow. Or this wasn't the same van.

But it had to be. And that Neanderthal upstairs just had to be the same Neanderthal who had jumped me at Jonsen's. Running into both Hulk and the van cinched it.

Especially added to the contents of the garage. Instead of the filthy, greasy pit you might expect, full of old auto parts salvaged from junkyards, this was a clean, tidy, cement-floored room, with crates and boxes stacked around. The garage was a damn warehouse! And not for used auto parts, either. This was where the ripped-off loot was stashed.

I wanted to let out a whoop of victory, but now wasn't the time. I could almost feel the adrenalin flowing into my veins. What you should do now, I told myself, is call Brennan and tell him to get out here and whip a John Doe warrant on these people and confiscate the goods and have that garbage living upstairs tossed into a more-or-less permanent can.

What I did instead was reach my hand through where the pane of glass used to be and unlock the window. I pushed it up and crawled inside. They call it breaking-and-entering, gang, and I just couldn't help myself.

Because I had to know.

I had to *know* it was the same van. I had to *know* those crates and boxes contained what I thought they contained.

Once inside, I walked softly and wished I had a big stick. There wasn't much light in here. Some little came through the open pane, and a single but fairly bright bulb was burning, hanging over a workbench affair built into the back wall, next to the open door of a toilet in the far corner. I felt fortunate at first that the bulb was lit, though on second thought its being on could easily mean someone would be coming back soon.

I started looking. The van, first. No way to be absolutely sure about it, but other than the license plates and the red lettering, it was a ringer, and I was convinced. I started poking into boxes, crates. Found everything from kitchen appliances to an antique vase. In one corner I found Mrs. Jonsen's grandfather clock, under a tarp. In another I found, crated up, her color TV.

In yet another I found, neatly boxed, the blue Christmas plates.

And for a quiet moment there, I was very angry.

Most of the stuff in the room was Mrs. Jonsen's. Not all, but most, and the way I figured it was these people moved out whatever they stole as quickly as possible. Mrs. Jonsen had been Thursday night and the stuff wasn't moved yet, but this was just Saturday, and with the van here, maybe tonight was the night. I didn't know what they did with their goods, but my guess was that they sold as much as possible to fences in the Quad Cities. Chicago wasn't that far away, either, and the not-easily-traced items (like a color TV with serial number "worn" away) could be fenced or sold locally. Antiques and such would have to be fenced outside of the area.

I'd seen enough.

I decided that, before leaving, it would be best for me to try to patch the window somehow, cover it up so they wouldn't notice anybody had broken in. But how? I remembered the workbench affair over under the hanging bulb; the workbench had a bunch of drawers down below, and I went over there and rummaged through them until I found black masking tape in one and a pile of rags in another, from which I selected a chuck of thick black cloth. I used scissors from another drawer to cut a square hole in the cloth.

I grinned. I was a genius. I would climb back out the window, close it shut, reach my hand up and in through the open pane and flip the lock, then tape the square piece of cloth over the empty space, stretching it taut and taping it tight. It was heavy cloth and, blended with the black of the rest of the window, would do as good a job as I could hope for keeping anybody in there from noticing the break-in for a time.

I tidied the workbench, got things put away and—still grinning, still proud of myself—I turned to go back across the big room to the window to tape the black cloth in place.

That was when I heard the shuffle of feet and voices, one saying, "Damnit! Look at the window over there! Somebody busted in!"

19

So there I stood: Mallory, master cat burglar, caught with my metaphorical pants down. My self-congratulatory thoughts fizzled out like wet firecrackers and were replaced with a rush of emotions, including terror, panic, and the ever-popular despair....

I blinked all that away.

Only for a split second had I allowed myself to wallow in self-pity and fear, but that was one split second too many in a situation as tight as this.

The rest of the second I used more wisely, used it to appraise the situation; the footsteps belonged to two people, it seemed, and they had entered through a doorway in the front of the building, a corner door directly opposite from where I was standing, back by the workbench. They hadn't seen me (and I hadn't seen them) because the view was blocked by the green van between us. But I couldn't think of making a dash for the window, which they had already noticed as being broken, and I wouldn't have had an ice-cube-in-hell of a chance to make it over there and not get caught, much less seen. Could I circle around the van and sneak out the door behind them?

"Lock that door up," one of the voices said.

Any other questions, Mallory?

"Already did," another voice said, with irritation that implied doing so was standard operating procedure. This was a high-pitched voice that belonged, I thought, to my old pal Hulk. He was saying, "Why so uptight about the door?"

"If somebody's in here, I don't want 'em getting out."

"I don't see nobody," Hulk observed.

"Probably just some goddamn neighbor kid broke the window to see what was in the big mystery garage. Well, we'll have a look-see anyway and make sure."

During that last exchange of dialogue, beginning at "Already did," I came to the conclusion that my only possible course of action was to duck into the lavatory that took up the corner nearest me next to the workbench. Before I did, I hastily opened up a drawer and traded the piece of black cloth and masking tape for that pair of scissors I'd used, then got shut soundlessly inside the can, all before the guys out there could get past the van to the point where they could see me.

Scissors in hand, I examined my cage. Like the outer, larger room of the garage, the john was not the pigsty you might be led to expect, judging from the exterior of the seedy-looking building. That doesn't mean you'd eat off the floor, but there were worse toilets in the world to have to make a home in. Seemed to be relatively clean, if not lavish: just bare facilities, standard stool and sink. Cramped it wasn't, and spaciously empty enough to suggest it had been designed with mechanics in mind, back in whatever era the place was used as a service garage; plenty of room to move around, not that I wouldn't have liked a dozen closets, two attic entries, and one trapdoor to a basement to hide in. Or at least a shower stall. But no, it was nothing more than a somewhat oversize naked can, with no place to hide unless you were very small and could tread water. No place at all.

Except maybe one.

A large cardboard box, big enough for a small stove, had been stuck in here to serve as an oversize wastebasket. Evidently, enough labor was still done in the garage to make necessary the frequent washing of hands: on the wall was a PULL DOWN, TEAR UP brown-paper towel dispenser, and the soap was strong, mechanic-strength powder in a dispenser over the sink, with the big carton apparently a spare liberated from warehouse duty to catch refuse.

Now I didn't want to make much noise, but figured the search for the intruder was going to lead here pretty soon, so I waited until I could hear a conversation going on out there, which I hoped would cover any sounds I'd make, and crawled into the box of wadded-up brown paper. Trying not to cause too much of a racket, and imagining every crinkle of paper to be a thunderclap, I squirmed and wriggled and swam in the sea of paper wads, getting a layer of the stuff over me.

It was not comfortable. Like I said before, the box was big enough for a small stove; but I am not shaped like a small stove. Also, most small stoves do not have two cracked ribs. Still, there I was, on my back in the box, my knees touching my chest, my arms around my legs, hugging, and my concentration going toward ignoring the pain, holding onto the scissors, and not breathing heavily.

I was like that for maybe two minutes, a bunched-up, awkward fetus clutching scissors in a box of crumpled towels, and then the john door burst open, like a fat man letting out air, and the light switched on and somebody came clumping in. I felt the box quiver as somebody gripped the side of it to peer in. I gripped the handle of the scissors. Tight.

"Nothing in here," the voice said. And it didn't sound like a voice with a wink in it, so I assumed I'd properly fooled the guy.

The door shut, and I was alone in the can again. And thankfully alone in my box. I wouldn't have liked any company; those used-up towels were obnoxious enough as it was.

Then I did something you will probably think is stupid, but I ask you to remember that everything I'd done for the past hour or so was pretty stupid, so as least I was consistent. What I did was carefully, as soundlessly as possible, get back out of the box so that I could approach the door and lay my ear to the wood and listen to the talk going on out there.

But the thing I heard was not talk. It was the sound of a door slamming. For a moment I wondered if those two guys had left, and then I got my answer. A new voice—an apparent third party who'd just entered—said, "I just talked to Frank, and I don't like it."

There was silence for a moment, then: "Me neither." My buddy Hulk talking. "I think Frank's going out on a limb on this one."

"Frank's going out on a limb? Bull," the new voice said. "*We* are the ones going out on the goddamn limb, not him."

The remaining voice, the authoritative voice belonging to the guy who spotted the broken window, said, "Take it easy. We'll be out of here by dawn, for Christ's sake. And Frank's right; we *should* cash in on *some* of our work at least, before we split. We laid the damn groundwork, and it'd be a pity to throw it away without making it pay off a little, anyway. I say go ahead."

"But in daylight?" This was the new voice again, the whiner.

"Why not? We done it in daylight before."

"But things weren't as hot before. That SOB Mallory wasn't sticking his puss into everything then."

"That's right," Hulk agreed, "and he came around here snooping this afternoon."

"What? Goddamn!" the whiner shouted.

"Forget Mallory," said the authoritative one, who'd evidently already been filled in by Hulk about my visit, whereas it seemed to be news to the whiner. "We can handle him. We got him covered."

Covered? What the hell did they mean by that?

"Well, even without Mallory, it's still hotter," the whiner said. "There's a murder in it now, and things are going to be hot and stay that way."

The authoritative voice was edged with anger this time. "I know that. Why do you think we're moving out tonight if I didn't know that?"

"I tell you, it bothers me," the whiner continued, trying a new tack. "I don't feel right about that old dead lady."

"For Christ's sake. Forget that old bitch."

"It's not that I give a damn about her, exactly; it's I *do* give a damn about getting stuck with a murder rap just because the old bag up and died on us."

"I'm getting sick of your goddamn complaining."

"Yeah? Well I'm getting sick of your goddamn orders. You're not running this show. Frank is."

"Well, Frank says we're going ahead with it. Right now."

"Well, the hell with Frank and the hell with you," the whiner said, a new toughness in his voice. "You and P. J. here can go ahead, but me, I'm going in the house and have a beer and see if I can cop a feel off P. J.'s woman. Let me know what happens."

I heard a door slam, and the other two guys started in grumbling. I strained to make it out, finally caught a piece of what the authoritative guy was saying—"Let's go talk to the stupid bastard"—and heard the door slam again.

I cracked the door of the can. Peeked out.

They were gone.

Gone back inside the house, I guessed.

I put the lid down on the toilet and sat, tried to get my heart working again, ran my fingers across my scalp to see if my hair was standing on end. Then I rose, ran some water in the sink, and splashed some on my face. It was good to be alive. It was good not to have any more cracked ribs than I already had; it was good not being kicked in the nuts.

I opened the lavatory door and walked back like a ballerina into the garage. My top priority was now to get the hell out of here and call Brennan. Obviously, going by what these guys had been saying, there was something on for tonight. Actually, a couple of somethings. It plainly sounded like they planned to get out of Port City by next morning, pack up and clear out.

But something else was up, too.

One last job, maybe? Groundwork was laid, the one guy had said, a pity to waste it. That had to be it, then: one last job, tonight.

On my way back over to the window, I stopped at the van. Out of almost idle curiosity, I tried the back doors of the van. Unlocked. I swung them open and looked in.

Empty.

That cinched it. Since they were planning to clear out of town by dawn, you would think the van would be loaded full of goodies. But no. Totally empty. Which meant one thing: there *was* one final farewell job planned for tonight. This van *would* be filled, but at some victim's house. By nightfall this vehicle would be crammed full of possessions and valuables earned and collected by somebody in a life of hard and probably honest work, only to be ripped off by some punks with a collective IQ in the neighborhood of Lee Trevino's average golf score.

I started closing the van doors, then stopped short.

Voices.

Voices outside the building, right outside the building, and the door was opening.

Damn! They were back already.

I ducked inside the van and closed the rear doors. Not all the way, but gently, so I could eventually nudge them open and hop out again when all was clear.

Sure.

"Well," the authoritative voice was saying, "screw him then. The two of us can do it."

"Hell, yes," Hulk said, uncertain.

And I heard a sound that had to be the garage door going up.

And another sound that had to be the rear doors of the van being pushed tight-shut.

And another that had to be the van's motor starting up.

We were moving.

20

It was dark in there. Not a trace of light was coming in around the edges of the double doors. No air, either. A hot, stuffy box; not an oven, but a damn close second; not a coffin, but just as disquieting. It was almost enough to make me homesick for that john back at the garage.

One thing kept me from tumbling into depression's abyss, and that thing was the pair of scissors. I sat clutching them as if they were a crucifix and I was expecting vampires.

Because it seemed inevitable that before long I'd be confronting those two guys driving the van, and if it hadn't been for those scissors, even *my* money would be on the van drivers. But having a weapon of sorts, and having the element of surprise on my side, gave me decent odds ... though stabbing somebody with a pair of scissors wasn't something I was looking forward to. After all, stabbing people with scissors was for psychos, and I was supposed to be one of the good guys.

However, at times one can't be too choosy about one's options, and I was lucky to have any option at all, and *damn* lucky to have something sharp and lethal with which to do battle against those dull and lethal boys up front in the van.

The shocks on the vehicle were all but nonexistent, and I've had smoother rides falling down a flight of stairs. But that too was a lucky break—and to hell with comfort—as since the ride was jostling and the vehicle naturally noisy, I didn't have to worry much about keeping down my own level of sound. Although when we went over those railroad tracks just three blocks from Tony's, I bounced around like a sack of grain and must've come within a hair of alerting my unknowing captors of my presence.

I examined the interior of the van and found nothing, not one thing, except some loose dirt on the slightly rusted-out floor. I went over the walls slowly, carefully, like a blind man reading braille—but not getting nearly as much out of it. A close check of the doors proved equally futile. The one on the right did have a square maintenance port near the latching mechanism, but feeling my fingers around in the hole told me nothing; perhaps if I had some slight mechanical know-how, it would've been different, but all I could get out of it was grease on my fingers. I considered prying the blades of the scissors around in there, but decided not to risk breaking them. I waited till we were going over a particularly bumpy stretch of road and, under cover of vehicle noise, laid my shoulder into the twin doors, hard. Nothing gave, except my shoulder. Some vans have doors that can be sprung open from within if you give 'em a shot right in the middle where they join; it's a very weak spot, from a structural point of view. But these doors—even though the van wasn't a recent model—were rugged and didn't budge. So I gave up.

I sat and let the rough-riding van knock my butt around, let it jounce me till my ribs hurt past pain. I deserved it for being idiotic enough to hide in a van in the first place. This is not to say that I was going to capitulate. I had given up on beating the van, but not on beating the van drivers. Those scissors were so tight in my fist, they could've been some strange, deadly deformity. I was tense with the knowledge of what was ahead of me. I was resolved to violence in a detached way like nothing I'd felt since Vietnam.

At first it was no trouble keeping track of where we were going. Even when my attention was focused on exploring my cell, I could perceive from the sounds of traffic that we were headed out of South End and into town. I felt the sway of the right turn past the pump factory and knew we'd be rolling down Mississippi Drive, and after maybe half a mile we turned again, left, into the downtown.

Then I got lost. Traffic sounds petered out, and several consecutive turns conspired to make me lose all sense of direction. We were, I supposed, winding through some residential area, God knew where. All I knew for sure was we weren't driving around on the bottom of the river.

And then we veered sharp to the right, and I could hear rocks spitting up against the underside of the vehicle, tickling the van's belly, and we came to a stop.

An alley, then. We'd stopped in an alley, probably in a residential area.

I heard the front van doors open, slam shut. No pretense at stealth. Had my presence been detected? I held the scissors ready, bayonetlike.

"What's going on up there?" I heard the authoritative voice say.

"Don't know," Hulk said. "Hell. Something."

"Something is right. I thought Frank said the college kids were gone on weekends."

"He did. He did say that."

"Well, they sure as hell aren't gone *this* weekend."

Silence.

Somebody put his hand on the handle that would open the rear van doors. From the positioning of the voices, I figured it was Hulk. I was ready. The scissors and I, we were ready.

He pushed down the handle with a click and began to pull open the doors.

"Wait," the authoritative voice said. "Hold it; somebody's coming."

I placed my foot against the right rear door along the bottom and put my hand inside the square opening. When Hulk pushed the doors shut, I kept the one door from latching by stopping it with my foot and bracing with my hand.

"How's it going, man?" A new voice. A young voice. And, I thought, a drunken voice. Or maybe stoned. You don't call two men "man" when your head is totally right.

"Fine," they said together.

"Going to do some gardening, man?"

"Yeah," they said.

"Well, uh … don't cut the grass *too* short, you know what I mean?" Laughter. His, not theirs. Silly laughter at that.

"Say," Authoritative Voice said, "what's going on anyway?"

"Party, man. Bash. Midsummer bash. Not many of us stuck around here for summer school, but whoever *is* around is upstairs, man. Hey, you want some beer or something?"

"No thanks," they said.

"Well, listen, if people start roamin' around outside while you're doing your work, man, don't mind 'em. Things aren't too hairy yet, but they're gettin' there. Party just got started last night. By tonight it really oughta be goin' good. Well, I gotta split."

"Good-bye," they said.

I heard his footsteps paddle away. A door yawned open, and I heard the sound of rock music blare out. Then it slammed and cut the music off.

"Damn," Hulk said.

"Goddamn," the other one said.

"What we going to do?"

"Scratch it."

"But...."

"No way we're going to get it done with all those kids wandering around, drunk on their butts, stoned out of their skulls. We were counting on it being the way Frank laid it out."

"Those goddamn college kids aren't supposed to be here on the weekend."

"Yeah. But they are. Let's go."

I heard their footsteps stirring up gravel and then the twin slams of the front van doors. The motor started up and, as they got moving again, I rolled out of the back of the van.

I hit hard, rolling off the alleyway into some bushes to my left. They hadn't seen or heard me.

They coasted away in the van, turning right at the mouth of the alley, and were gone.

I got to my feet, brushed myself off, and looked around.

Across the alley from where I stood was a two-story yellow clapboard house. It was set up a slight incline to a basement garage. Upstairs was where the party was going on. In the second-story windows I could see the young bodies moving around; and now the sound of rock music, inaudible in the van except when that door had opened, was easy to hear. And strangely out of place in this sleepy residential area full of sedate old two-story houses like this one.

Which was, by the way, a house I recognized.

It was where the Cooper sisters lived.

21

As quietly as possible, I brushed aside the questions of the Cooper sisters, and got their permission to use the phone, and dialed the sheriff's office. Lou Brown answered.

"How's it going, Mal? Can I help?"

"It's gone past that point, Lou. I'm ready to bring Brennan in."

"You been moving fast, then. I thought you were going to keep me up on what you were doing."

"Well, I hadn't done a damn thing till this afternoon, and now it's broken loose all at once. Is Brennan around?"

"He's sacked out upstairs. He was out till all hours on an accident call last night."

"Bother him."

"That important, huh?"

"That important."

"Okay."

I heard the click of the extension button being punched in, and it took ten rings to get Brennan to answer. Good thing he wasn't a fireman.

"What is it?" he said, very groggy.

"It's Mallory. Wake up."

"Oh, Jesus. I was out late, Mallory, have a heart. Trying to catch some sleep, damn it; can't you talk to Lou or somebody about whatever it is—"

"Brennan, wake up. I got your break-ins solved for you."

"You what?"

"Know a place called Tony's Used Auto Parts?"

He sighed. "Down in South End, sure."

"Well, the garage part of Tony's is a warehouse for the hot goods these guys rip off. It's where they keep the stuff till they can get it fenced."

"Mallory, I don't know how to tell you this, but we've heard the same rumors about Tony's that you have, and on my say-so the cops used two John Does on that place in the last five weeks, and they never found a damn thing. We've pushed our luck on that one about as far as we can. So no matter what you heard about Tony's, forget it."

"I didn't *hear* anything about Tony's, Brennan ... I *saw* it."

"What? What do you mean?"

"Just what I said. I busted in there this afternoon and had a look around."

"Goddamnit, Mallory! You can't—"

"Can't, hell. I did. Now do you want to tell me how you're going to toss me in the can and so on, or do you want to hear what I found out?"

Another sigh. "Go on."

"I only saw one of them. A big guy, with a blond crew cut and a broken nose. He's the one that clobbered me at Mrs. Jonsen's when I interrupted him loading up that green van. His name is P. J., I think, and I believe he lives above the auto parts shop with some woman, who's probably in on it, too. The others I didn't see, but I heard 'em talking. The main guy wasn't around, but they referred to him as Frank."

"You're out of your mind, Mallory. Breaking in there, eavesdropping, *damn*—"

"Shut up and listen. They've got all the stuff they stole from Mrs. Jonsen's, everything from her color television to her antiques, still stored away in that garage. But from what they were saying, I gather they're going to skip town tonight, and I wouldn't be surprised if they're loading that stuff into that green van I told you about right this minute, so move it, will you?"

"Well … it's within the city limits, so I'll have to call the chief of police and have him get some men down there straight away. If they use another warrant on that place and don't find anything, the chief'll have my ass and I'll have yours."

"Just do it."

"Where are you now?"

I gave him the number.

"Well, sit tight there, Mallory. I'll get back to you in a minute."

I hung up.

And as I did, Miss Viola Cooper handed me a crystal glass filled with that delicious homemade dandelion wine, and Miss Gladys Cooper said, "Now come into the living room and tell us what this is all about."

I followed them into the cluttered living room, sat on the sofa, and sipped my wine. They had good reason to wonder what I was doing there; not only had I come around on a Saturday afternoon, rather than my traditional Thursday evening with their hot suppers, but I was also a scraped-up, dirty, disheveled sight from my tumble out of the van in their alley, and I still had the pair of scissors clutched in my hand, I laid them on a doily-strewn end table by the sofa and told the sisters that I had just been witness to the kids who lived upstairs preventing the robbery of the Cooper home by two bogus gardeners.

The old girls didn't bat an eye. Gladys said, "That doesn't surprise me. Our roomers are nice young men. I don't know why old folks are always criticizing you nice, responsible young people."

Viola said, "We've already spoken to Mr. Mallory on that subject, Gladys."

That they had—several times.

"It's a point worth stressing," Gladys said. "How did the boys prevent the robbery?"

"By being here," I explained. "Evidently, the thieves had information to the effect that your roomers usually aren't here on the weekend."

"That is true," Viola said. "But this weekend they *are* here …"

"… having a party," her sister continued. "I don't know if you noticed that or not."

If I hadn't, the ceiling above—rattling with the vibrations of dancing feet and booming stereo—would have clued me in. But the sisters didn't seem to notice or mind.

"Are these the same people who robbed and killed that poor Mrs. Jonsen?" Gladys asked me.

"And weren't you present at the scene of that robbery as well?" her sister added.

I nodded yes. "And I know what you're thinking. It couldn't just be a coincidence. But don't ask me how it figures in, because I don't know."

"Mrs. Jonsen was participating in the Hot Supper Service," Gladys said, "just as we are, and …"

"... couldn't that be the common element between these dreadful robberies?" her sister finished.

"These same people pulled seven other break-ins locally," I said, "and the Hot Supper Service didn't turn up in any of them."

"I see," Viola said. "More wine?"

"Please."

She filled my crystal glass, and her sister asked, "How did they intend to rob us?"

I explained that the way I saw it, the thieves were planning to pull their van into the basement garage, come upstairs, tie the sisters up (as they had Mrs. Jonsen), and carry what they took back downstairs, and load up the van.

"And they can do things like that in the daylight?" Viola asked.

Gladys said, "Of course, because people just don't like to get involved these days, do they, Mr. Mallory?"

"Most of them have sense enough not to," I said.

At that point the phone rang. It was for me: Brennan, calling to tell me he'd contacted the police and was on his way to meet them down at Tony's. I said, "Something else you should consider, Brennan."

"What's that?"

"This afternoon, these guys were planning to rip off some nice elderly ladies named Gladys and Viola Cooper but got fouled up, never mind why. The main thing is the Cooper sisters are one of my Hot Supper charges."

"You mean like Mrs. Jonsen was?"

"Right."

"That's kind of a strange sort of coincidence, isn't it?"

"Isn't it? The Cooper sisters themselves mentioned it to me a moment ago, and I shrugged it off. But remember how we were looking for a common factor among the break-ins? Like that travel agency that figured in on several of them. And how we considered the possibility of maybe this bunch utilizing several sources of information?"

"You mean the travel agency is one source, and the Hot Supper thing another, somehow?"

"Worth thinking about. Anyway, one thing's for sure."

"Yeah?"

"We got another common factor."

"Yeah," he said. "You."

"Me," I agreed.

Brennan hung up. So did I.

Or began to, anyway, because hardly had receiver touched cradle when Viola Cooper said, "Perhaps you're wrong."

I let the receiver drop onto the hook, turned around and looked at the two sisters, standing there side by side like a matched set. How long they'd been poised behind me like that, in the hallway where the phone was on a stand, I didn't know—and didn't care, really. It was their house, after all, and they were the ones who'd almost gotten robbed. Why shouldn't they be interested?

"I'm wrong?" I said. "What do you mean?"

"Maybe you are not the common factor, Mr. Mallory," Gladys Cooper said. "Or at least not the only one. My sister and I were talking while you were on the phone. We have an idea."

I grinned. "What have you come up with, ladies?"

"As much as we hate to say it ...," Gladys began.

"... because they are all such nice people," her sister continued.

"... it seems to us that one of the *other* persons who brings our hot suppers might be the common factor, rather than you, Mr. Mallory."

"Hey," I said. "That's right. I only bring the food around on Thursday nights. ..."

"And the other six nights of the week, it's brought to us by other Hot Supper volunteers," Gladys pointed out, finishing *my* sentence this time, "volunteers who service the very same route that you do."

"And isn't it possible," her sister continued, "that one of these other parties might have been using the Hot Supper delivery to ... I believe the phrase is 'case the joint'? Not to impugn anyone's humanitarian intentions...."

"Do you suspect anyone in particular?" I asked them. They were doing fine so far.

Gladys shook her head. "All of them *seem* so sincere, it's difficult to—"

"Now wait a moment," Viola said. It was the first time I'd heard her break in to offer a new thought, rather than just complete one of her sister's. "Couldn't it be that young couple who were delivering the Thursday meals before Mr. Mallory began?"

I said, "The people I took over for, you mean?"

"Yes," Viola said.

"But they seemed so warm and conscientious," Gladys said. "I can't believe that they—"

Her sister was firm. "Then why did they drop out of the program so early? They delivered meals for no longer than a month, do you recall? That was one of the reasons we were so surprised to see Mr. Mallory bringing our Thursday meals."

Gladys was starting to nod in agreement. "And their business would provide a natural means for disposing of the property they procure. I believe you're right, Viola."

I said, "What business is that?"

"Why, they're antique dealers," Viola said. "Of a sort, anyway. Their shop is somewhat run-down … nothing fancy; the place almost resembles a junkyard. It's just outside the city limits out of South End; perhaps you've seen it…."

"They just bought the place a few months ago, late last spring," Gladys recalled. "They explained to us that they have plans to refurbish the shop and the grounds, as well as that barn of theirs, when their financial situation improves."

Barn! Another warehouse?

I said, "What are their names?"

"Petersen," Gladys said.

"Frank and Sarah Petersen," Viola said.

22

"Damn it, Mallory," Brennan said, "you ought to have enough sense not to come butting in down here." Harsh words, but considering the source, not much of a reprimand. Brennan was pleased with me, for a change, and pleased with the haul I'd helped him make. Behind him the garage door of Tony's Used Auto Parts was up, and visible in there were the boxes and crates containing the ripped-off goods from Mrs. Jonsen's, waiting patiently to be confiscated and marked as evidence. Not so patient was the uniformed cop keeping watch over the stuff, hand on holstered gun, ready to blast the first box that blinked; he'd be better when the chief and chief's inspector showed up to get the red-tape ball rolling. Another uniformed cop was sitting behind the wheel of a blue-and-white parked up on the sidewalk in front of the shop half of the building; in the backseat, sulking, was the pale, dark-haired woman who'd shown me a sliver of face when I knocked on the upstairs door earlier that afternoon, and she was prettier than you might expect of a woman who lived with Hulk (aka P. J.). Brennan was standing beside his own unit, which was nosed in behind the blue-and-white. Mine was across the street in that parking lot behind the Little League ballpark—my blue van, I mean. I was there to pick it up. I told Brennan so.

"That's no excuse for coming down here. You should've waited till later, when things died down. You want to blow the whole thing?"

I didn't understand why I would blow the whole thing by being here, after I handed the thing silver-platter-style to him and his friends in blue. But I didn't bother mentioning that to Brennan, instead saying, "Come on, walk me over to my car. I got something I want to tell you."

He said okay, and we picked our way through the heavy five o'clock traffic flowing by Tony's. On the way over, he explained that when the warrants were filled in, I'd been listed as "long-time, reliable informant," a designation that carried with it certain rights of anonymity, which in turn carried with it a vagueness beneficial to rule-bending, underhanded police activities. And if I came around and tipped to somebody (like that pale girl in the back of the police unit) that *I* was the "long-time, reliable informant" who had gathered his information via breaking-and-entering, well, then....

But I didn't care about any of that; I was still preoccupied with working on the new information given me by the Cooper sisters. All the way down here in the back of the taxi, I'd been going over what I had so far, my mind sorting slowly through the various file cards, wheezing and clanking like the world's oldest and most inefficient computer. Picking up the van hadn't been my only reason for returning to Tony's, of course. More important was my telling Brennan about Frank and Sarah Petersen.

"Who?" Brennan said.

We were leaning against my van now. Across the way the dilapidated, ill-formed building with its black-painted windows provided a surreal backdrop for the rush-hour traffic flowing by.

"Frank and Sarah Petersen," I said. "They have an antique shop outside of town a ways...."

"Oh yeah! Used to be old man Benson's for years. These Petersens—are they the young couple who bought the place last spring?"

"Right. Brennan, I'm positive Frank Petersen is the organizer behind the break-ins. Remember, I heard P. J. and the two others mention the name Frank, and the antique thing is a perfect front; they even have a barn out there, which surely serves the same purpose the garage at Tony's does."

"That's pretty thin to risk a warrant on. Lots of guys in the world are named Frank, you know, and there's no law against antique shops, or barns either."

"Let me get the rest of it out, will you, Brennan?" But I hesitated, not knowing how much to say about Debbie Lee and her husband Pat Nelson.

Damn! Even now I separated them in my mind ... Debbie Lee and her husband Pat Nelson ... but could there be any doubt that Debbie had suckered me in, sucked me in, fucked me in, led me into screwing her when she was really screwing me, keeping me busy for her husband while he and his fellow rip-off artists got their shit together and got out of town ... helping convince me, with that drunken husband story and that stairwell confrontation, that Pat was just a jealous hot-head, a paranoid yes, but certainly not one of the bastards who robbed and killed Mrs. Jonsen ... because after all, if Pat *was* one of those people, would he have risked fighting me and pulling a knife on me and all? The brazenness of that was calculated to make me rule Pat out—even if his red-white-and-blue GTO *had* been at the scene of the crime—rule him out for the time being anyway, and since they were planning to split soon, the time being was plenty; because the time being would be filled with me staying at Debbie's side to protect her from her drunken, violent husband. "We got him covered," they'd said this afternoon. Covered was right: under the covers with Pat Nelson's wife. Yes, Debbie Lee had done it to me again. Damn.

But I didn't tell Brennan about that. I wasn't ready. And anyway, I had plenty more to tell him. Like that Frank and Sarah Petersen were the Hot Supper couple who had preceded me on the route that included both Mrs. Jonsen and the Cooper sisters.

"That's it, then!" he said, excited. "We were right about them using several different sources of information. The Hot Supper thing was one, and another was Bill Morgan's travel agency."

"What? What travel agency did you say?"

"You know. You commented yourself that it was the only agency in town. Bill Morgan, the attorney, owns it."

William Morgan. The attorney that Debbie said she worked for. I had assumed she was his legal secretary, which I should've known was ridiculous, considering her lack of training. She had, no doubt, worked not in his law office, but in his travel agency. I told Brennan. Told him I had good reason to believe that the leak in Morgan's agency was a woman named Debbie Nelson.

"And," I said, "she and her husband are good friends of Frank and Sarah Petersen. As a matter of fact, I saw Debbie Nelson and Sarah Petersen together just this morning."

"This Debbie Nelson … she isn't….?"

"She is. Pat Nelson's wife. The same Pat Nelson whose GTO, license number three, was outside of Mrs. Jonsen's that night. And something else."

"Don't stop now."

"That van. That green van. It had the words 'GARDENING SERVICE' on its side. Evidently, one of the ways they've kept from raising suspicion on daylight break-ins is by posing as gardeners."

"I already have an APB out on the van. I'll have that added to the description."

"Good, but wait a minute; I'm still not through. Pat Nelson works for a nursery, and that means the gardening bit could be more than just words painted on a van."

"Sure," Brennan said, nodding. "It could be another source of information. A regular gardening service would have access to plenty of information as to when people are and are not going to be home. You wouldn't happen to know which nursery Nelson works for?"

I thought for a moment. "I believe a guy named Chet Richards runs it." That was the name Debbie had told me, anyway.

"Are you kidding?"

"Of course not."

"Hell, Mallory, you know who Richards is?"

"No. Who is he?"

"Well, for openers, that pale little girl in the backseat over there is Felicia Richards. Chet's her brother."

"You're kidding."

"No, I'm not, Mallory. We've had run-ins with Richards and his sister before. I tried to nail him for pushing dope last year, and word is that nursery of his is an investment made from several years of pushing. And he was pimping, too. Used to sit down at the Old Mill Bar and pimp for guess who?"

"Who?"

"Felicia. His sister."

"Nice, I like a family business.'

"Well, Mallory, looks like it's all fitting together. Looks like if I can collar these people, we'll have a case against them."

"Looks that way."

"Mallory, I want to tell you something."

"Go ahead, Brennan."

"I want to tell you thanks. Thanks for—well, damn it—thanks for not paying any attention to me when I told you to stay out of this thing. You've done a lot."

"Not really. Most of it came from these people knowing me and worrying that maybe I'd recognized them, or maybe start poking my nose around. They blew their cool, probably because they hadn't planned on anything like murder entering in."

"Just the same. Thanks." He put his hand out.

"Why shouldn't I shake hands with my best friend's father?" I said. And did.

He turned and crossed the still busy street and walked over to the cop in the blue-and-white and gave him several minutes of instructions. Then he got in his own unit, turned his siren on, and cleared a space in the line of traffic; once in, he switched off the siren and headed out of town, south: out toward the antique shop run by Frank and Sarah Petersen.

I wished I was going with him, in a way.

And in another way, I was glad I was out of it. Glad it was over for me. My gut tightened when I thought about Pat Nelson and the mentality that let him callously rip people off, rob them of their property, from their prized possessions, like antique Christmas plates, to that most prized possession of all: life.

And Debbie? It would be a while before I could even think about her at all, even in a negative way. She had always been a scarred area on my psyche, but nothing severe—more like a shallow pit on your skin where you once popped a pimple when you were thirteen. But this time, her wound had cut deep, and when scar tissue finally covered the area over, it would leave an ugly place.

I got in my van, anxious to get home, to crawl back into the wonderful solitary confinement of my ancient silver trailer, to drink a six-pack or two of Pabst and fall into oblivious, drunken sleep that would, I hoped, be dreamless. But the traffic was thick and snail-paced, and I had to head up West Hill to avoid it, through residential districts; then I could cut down Second Street and on up East Hill and home. The West Hill detour took me past Mrs. Fox's place, and I slowed as I drove by, glancing at her stately but now declining two-story gray nineteenth-century home, wondering how the nice old gal was doing. Parked on her slanted, well-tended lawn, backed up to the side entrance of the house, was a van.

A green van with the words GARDENING SERVICE on the side.

23

The house next door was smaller than Mrs. Fox's, but of the same gothic, dignified type, and seemed in less of a state of decline. My insistent knocking was answered by a man of perhaps sixty-five, wearing an obviously expensive ash gray suit that indicated he was still active in business; he was thin without looking frail, with hair the same color as his suit and a long face whose deep lines were presently deepened further in irritation. He hadn't even finished asking who the hell I was when I pushed my way in and closed the door behind me.

"What do you think you're doing," he sputtered, frightened now, "barging into a person's house—get out of here before I call the police!"

"That's just what I want you to do," I said.

I gave him a second to say, "What...?" and calm down a bit.

Then I excused myself for barging in and explained about the robbery next door. I was just finishing up as a handsome, silver-haired woman in a beige dress appeared at the mouth of the entryway; she was a few years older than her husband. "What's the fuss, Henry? Who is this young man?"

"He says there's a robbery going on next door, Genevieve."

"Good heavens! Is it that green van pulled up to the house?"

I nodded, getting impatient, wishing these people would get a move on.

"I thought that was suspicious," she said. "She always has her son do the gardening for her. She can't afford having it done. Are these the same people who killed that poor Mrs. Jonsen?"

I nodded again and said, "And no doubt they're holding Mrs. Fox captive right now."

The man said, "I'll phone the police at once," and rushed off. Finally!

His wife was shaking her head back and forth, saying, "I just don't understand people anymore, I really don't."

"Ma'am," I said, "do you have a back door?"

"Yes, of course."

"Could I use it?"

"Yes, of course. I'll show you the way."

But first I had to step back onto their front porch for a moment to retrieve something: a tire iron I'd gotten from my van, the best short-notice weapon I could come up with. I didn't intend to lay my ribs on the line again without some protection. I'd left it out of sight on the porch before knocking, as I hadn't wanted to alarm these people any more than necessary. Now that they understood the situation, my being armed wouldn't shock them, even if my weapon was somewhat unorthodox.

So I slipped out the back and was glad to be able to avoid coming up on the van from the street side; this way, cutting through the neighbors' yard and up the hill on the passenger's side of the vehicle, my approach was less obvious, more unexpected. I moved quietly but not slowly—in a crouch, like a humorless Groucho Marx, holding onto the tire iron with two hands, as if I were expecting somebody to try and take it away. There was no sound coming from the van: no voices, no shuffle of feet, no scrape of objects being moved. At first I thought they were just being extra-cautious in their loading, but even when

I got right up next to the van, there was nothing but silence within. Either the van was already full and the two guys were inside the house having a final look around; or the van was empty and the loading hadn't begun yet. The latter made more sense to me, but that doesn't mean I eased my grip on the tire iron, though it did give me the courage to go squeezing through the space between van and house.

Nobody there.

Nothing in the van.

Meaning they hadn't started loading yet; they weren't far enough along with the heist for that. Which made sense. After all, they were short-handed; only two of them had gone along. That one guy, the whining one, had decided to stay behind. Damn! I should've guessed when the guys in the van struck out at the Coopers' place that they'd go on ahead and try Mrs. Fox's—the groundwork had been laid, they'd said; why waste it? I would've kicked myself in the butt if I'd had the time and energy to spare.

I moved around to the front of the van, opened the door on the passenger's side, and got a nice surprise. The keys were in the dash. One key stuck in the ignition, the other (the rear-door key) dangling like an earring in poor taste. I yanked them out of the dash and dropped them in my pocket; our two rip-off artists wouldn't be leaving in this van, not unless they cared to go coasting down the hill in neutral. The thought of that made me smile and helped chip away at my tension, my apprehension; started to loosen me up. I'd been too late to help Mrs. Jonsen, but, damnit, the cavalry was going to be on time this trip.

Between the two seats was a big box of gardener's tools, probably containing its share of burglary tools, too, if you cared to dig deep enough. I didn't, but the top level of the box provided me with several items I felt would prove useful: a piece of grease-smeared cloth, the stuff that gags are made of; and a coil of rope, probably the remainder of a larger coil of rope, part of which had been used to tie up Mrs. Jonsen last Thursday. And it was no trick to guess what use a similar length of rope had been put to in the past few minutes.

I returned to the rear of the van and glanced in the open side door of the house. A half flight of stairs rose to a landing and a closed door. I stuck my head inside for a closer look, and somebody behind that closed door said, "I'll get started, Chet."

It was a distant voice, but not *that* distant, and I once again ducked inside the van's rear compartment. That van's rear end was getting to be a second home for me, and I huddled in its darkest corner, hiding in its deep shadows, the tire iron in my hands like a rifle. A plan of sorts had started to form in my head, having partially to do with the rag I'd stuffed in my pocket and the coil of rope slung over my shoulder. I waited for the distant voice to get closer.

Didn't take long. The door at the top of that half flight of stairs popped open, like it had been butted open, which in fact it had. Hulk (or P. J., or whatever the hell you want to call him) came down the stairs, arms filled with a big box that blocked his vision.

So. After the Cooper score had fizzled, they'd gone back to Tony's to get some boxes so they could pack up Mrs. Fox's antiques carefully, on the scene; since they planned to cut out tonight, that would save time. And that accounted for why they weren't any further along with the robbery than they were. They must've got out of Tony's just a whisker before Brennan and the cops made the scene.

P. J. ducked into the van. He put his load down near the front, his back to me, and though that big ass of his made a damn tempting target, I had something better in mind. There's a streak of revenge in the best of us, you know, and I swung that shaft of iron into his side, into his ribcage, and at the same time covered his mouth with my left hand, a hand now holding that greasy rag. Once I had the rag stuffed in his mouth, I let him turn himself around, still doubled over with pain; he took one look at the tire iron and, out of reflex action, stood up straight.

Which is something you don't want to do inside a van, especially when you're Hulk's size. But he did it anyway and, in doing so, banged his head into the roof of the van like a hammer driving in a nail, making a *thunk* sound that echoed hollowly in the small compartment. He fell to his knees, then on his face. He couldn't have been out colder if I had bashed him in the head with the tire iron.

I used the rope to tie his hands and feet together behind him, in one big package. He was breathing well, despite the greasy rag crammed in his mouth, and as long as he didn't choke to death on the taste of the thing, he'd be okay; besides, he wouldn't be waking up for a while anyway.

After I locked the van's rear doors, I tossed the keys over into a hedge in the neighbors' yard. I figured that was as good a place as any for them. Then the tire iron and I walked back around the van, entered the house, and crept up the stairs to the landing, cracking open the door to see what was beyond, ready to cave in the first unfriendly skull that presented itself.

Fortunately, what was beyond the door was the kitchen, with not an unfriendly skull in sight. It was big, a high-ceilinged ballroom of a kitchen, with light pine cabinets surrounding the room and gleaming white walls showing beneath them. Two of the walls were lined with ancient but well-preserved appliances: multiple-burner gas range, big round-shouldered Westinghouse, long horizontal freezer you could store a buffalo in, with an electric dishwasher the only apparent recent addition. Otherwise the room was empty, with the exception of the small, square pine table and its chairs in the center of the room. Sitting at the table, tied to one of those chairs and gagged, was Mrs. Fox.

She was wearing what she'd worn that first evening I'd brought her hot supper around—a blue cotton dress with white cameo brooch—and was maintaining her usual quiet dignity. She seemed to be waiting, with patience, and with some irritation, for these intruders to be done with their sacking of her home and leave her alone.

Her eyes smiled when she saw me, and when I took the gag off, I saw the corresponding smile below. But she was a smart old gal and didn't say a word as I untied her. I whispered, "Go out the side here, and go over to the house next door. The police are on their way."

And she whispered back at me, "You'll have to help me to the door. My cane is in the living room, and I'll never make it without support."

"What about after you get outside?"

"Then I'll crawl if I have to. I just don't feel that my falling down in here and causing a commotion would be ideal, do you?"

I walked her over to the door and helped her on down the steps and out of the house, as carefully as an usher at a wedding seating the mother of the bride. Once outside, however, I realized she'd had an ulterior motive in asking for my aid. She said, still whispering, "Now listen here, young man, you just come along with me; you're not going back inside that house."

"I have to."

"You said the police are coming," she said. "Let them take care of this. You stay away from those people in there. Don't go in that house."

"I have to."

That was when the old guy from next door appeared and took Mrs. Fox by the arm and began walking her over to his place. She kept her eyes on me, however, her expression making it clear she didn't approve of my going back in.

But I did anyway, of course, and my first action was to kick over the chair Mrs. Fox had been sitting tied-up in. It clattered to the floor, and the noise brought on the hoped-for response; I heard movement out in the other part of the house and positioned myself to the right of the swinging kitchen door, and when somebody pushed through, I cut him in half with the tire iron.

"Sh … i … i … it," he gushed, the air emptying out of him.

His was a voice from this afternoon, the voice of the guy who had seemed second-in-command to the as-yet-unseen Frank Petersen. He was short, dark-haired, and lean, and he wore dark green gardener's coveralls with a conspicuous lump in the right pocket. The lump was shaped like a small automatic. He was pale and had a more than superficial resemblance to the girl I'd seen at Tony's. This, then, was Chet Richards, friend and accomplice of Pat Nelson, pimp and brother of Felicia Richards.

"You!" he said. "Mallory! You son of a…."

He didn't finish, because I raised the tire iron as if to strike, and he covered his head and cowered.

"Nice meeting you, Chet," I said. "But then we've met before, right?"

"Where's the old lady? Where's P. J.?"

"P. J. wanted to be here, but he got all tied up. And I sent the old lady someplace where no one's trying to kill her."

"Listen, nobody meant to kill that other old broad."

"Shut up. I don't think I want to hear that line of bullshit when I don't have to. You just keep quiet, Chet."

"What ... what are you going to do?"

"Wait. I'm going to wait for just a few minutes for the cops to get here."

"Cops?"

"That's right. I already called them. It's all over."

Something got going in his eyes. Thoughts of the gun in his coverall pocket, most likely.

"Don't even think about it, Chet. As close as I am anyway to opening you up with this tire iron, you just don't want to push me."

And the door behind me swung open hard, knocking me over, sending the tire iron pitching from my hand. I reached out after it, but the guy kicked the iron across the room, then came back and stepped on my hand, grinding my fingers like they were grapes and he was making wine.

"Well, look who the hell it is," Pat Nelson said.

His voice sounded different than it had the other night in the stairwell when he was doing his Dean Martin parody. But it *was* a voice I recognized; I'd heard it back at Tony's, and at Mrs. Jonsen's, and one night outside my trailer. Pat had been the third party—the whiner—the guy who'd stayed behind at the garage before the Cooper job. But evidently, when Chet and P. J. went back to the garage after that fell through, they'd talked Pat into coming along to Mrs. Fox's. That was something else I should've figured, damnit! After all, Felicia Richards had been alone when Brennan and the cops had raided Tony's; there'd been no sign of the whiner. I should've considered the possibility of his being here. Damn.

"Mallory," Pat said, "I tell you, you got to be the craziest goddamn bastard I ever run across, you know that? Why do you cause so much goddamn misery for you and everybody else?" He too was in green coveralls, but his gun was in hand, not in pocket. It was a little thing, an automatic sized to fit a woman's purse, and it was ridiculous that it scared me as much as it did.

"Never mind that, Pat," Chet said, scrambling onto his feet. "The cops are on the way; we got to get the hell out of here."

Pat's face narrowed, and he came over and called me a bastard again and kicked me in the ribs. Not a very forceful kick, really, but it didn't take much; pain shot through me like a flare, and I blacked out for a moment.

When I came to, I pushed up on one elbow and looked around. They were gone. I wondered for how long.

Then Pat told me. His voice, from outside, was saying: "Where are the goddamn keys! What did he do with the god-damn car keys!"

By the time they reentered, I had managed to crawl over to the tire iron and get hold of it. I pitched the thing at Pat; I missed by a mile. He grabbed me by the shirt front, heaved me off the floor, and stuck his gun in my Adam's apple. "What did you do with them, Mallory? What did you do with the goddamn keys?"

"I left them with your wife," I said, "the last time I had her."

That was not the sanest thing I might've said; it got me slapped with the automatic and thrown back to the floor.

"Hey, what he said," Chet said. "Your wife, you had her listening, right? She had to hear the squeal on the radio, right? She ought to be on her way."

Meaning Pat had a police-band radio; either at home or rigged up inside his GTO, or both. No big deal; anybody can buy a radio like that—or steal one—and they prove quite useful to guys in Pat's line of work.

"Let's hope she beats the cops here," Pat said.

"Come on," Chet said. "We'll head down the hill—that's the way she'll be coming."

"First I ought to shoot that bastard—"

"Never mind him; come on!"

"Mallory," Pat said, "I ought to blow your head off, you know that? But I'm going to prove something to you. We told you we didn't mean to off that old broad, told you we weren't no goddamn murderers, and I'm going to prove we aren't by letting you keep your goddamn worthless skin. What do you think of that?"

"Will you quit wasting time?" Chet said, and yanked Pat by the arm.

Pat gave me one last foul look, and they left.

I pushed up on my hands, then hands and knees, and then got on my feet. My legs were wobbly and my vision blurry, but I managed to navigate myself toward the door, and finally I was down the steps and outside, leaning against the van. Half a block away, Pat Nelson and Chet Richards were jogging, jogging easy toward the red-white-and-blue GTO double-parked across the street. I don't have to tell you who was behind the wheel. Debbie's apartment was only a few blocks away, and so of course she beat the police here. A wave of helplessness washed through me; she and Pat and Chet would get away clean now, wouldn't they? Some goddamn cavalry I was.

Then I noticed Lou.

Sometime in the last thirty seconds or so, Lou Brown had pulled up in front of Mrs. Fox's in one of the Sheriff's Department units, and now he was standing there in his cream-colored uniform, watching Chet and Pat approach the GTO and, apparently, trying to figure out what the hell was going on.

"Lou!" I hollered. "Get those guys!"

He turned and saw me, and something odd floated across his face. Then he looked away from me and back toward the jogging figures and yelled, "Halt!" His voice was quavering; he was scared shitless.

Pat and Chet both stopped dead, glanced at Lou for a moment, glanced at each other and exchanged confused grins, then resumed their jogging. They were just a few feet from the GTO now and didn't seem worried.

They should've been.

Lou had drawn his big, long-barreled .357 Magnum and, both hands entwined around the butt, both fingers on the trigger, he yelled again, "Halt!"

And fired.

Chet did a jerky ballet movement as the bullet hit, blood spurting from him, and he flopped onto his back on the pavement. He had a surprised look on his face, frozen there now, and Pat had a similar look of surprise on his face as he looked down at his dead friend. He swung around, automatic in hand, and said, "What...?"

And Lou fired again.

Red spurted out the front of Pat's chest and splattered against the side of the GTO, and he did his own jerky ballet movement and joined Chet.

Debbie's blonde hair caught a glint of the dying sun as she tumbled out of the GTO and cradled her husband's head in her lap, sitting there with him in the street. She rocked him like she was easing a baby off to sleep, but the job was already done. Pat was as asleep as you can get.

24

Lou covered his mouth with one hand and holstered the big revolver with the other. I joined him. His eyes were red, wet, shifting rapidly as if to avoid seeing me or anybody or anything. He said, "Jesus ... what else could I do? They had guns."

The stench of cordite was making me sick. I breathed through my mouth.

Lou said, "What else could I do, Mal?"

I shrugged.

I walked over to Debbie. She didn't look up at me, but she knew I was there. She wasn't crying yet. She said, "I'm sorry, Mal." Tiny voice.

"Me too, Debbie."

"Will there be an ambulance soon?"

"Yes."

"Not that an ambulance would do him any good. I just don't want him in the street like this."

"Can I do anything, Debbie?"

"No."

"Okay."

"Mal?"

"Yeah?"

"Thank you ... for ... not hating me."

"I couldn't hate you, Debbie."

"Don't let Lou get away with this, Mal. He's going to have to answer for this."

I wasn't quite sure what she meant, but I said, "I won't," to soothe her.

And so I walked back over to Lou, who was standing with a hand over his mouth and another on the butt of the holstered gun, his face especially pale, his black sideburns and thin mustache looking pasted on, unreal. In the background, porches and lawns were filling with people: people who'd heard the cannon blasts of the .357 Magnum, people standing with looks of detached horror on their faces as they viewed the two torn bodies that lay in the street.

The guy who lived next door to Mrs. Fox, the gray-haired, gray-suited old businessman, joined us for a moment to say that he'd called for an ambulance.

"And," he said, "Mrs. Fox would like to know if she can go home now. She says she has a lot of straightening up to do."

"I don't see why not," Lou said.

The old guy nodded and turned to go. Then he added, "Oh, and you, young man … your name is Mallory?"

"Yes."

"Mrs. Fox said to tell you you were a fool to go back in there … but a nice fool, and she wants to thank you personally and would like to know if you could stop over to see her before you go?"

"Tell her sure."

He returned to his home, and we watched while he brought Mrs. Fox by the arm down his porch steps and walked her back to that same side entrance of her house. Before she went in, she turned to smile at me, and I found a smile to throw back to her.

But I couldn't make the smile last long.

Because somewhere in my head, somewhere I was finally putting it all together. The information had been there the whole time, but I hadn't seen the pattern; I hadn't assorted the file cards in their correct, most revealing order. What Debbie had said to me—and the frozen looks of surprise on the faces of the husks that had been Pat Nelson and Chet Richards—made it all make sense.

"Was killing them the only way, Lou?"

"I was just trying to stop them," he said. "I didn't mean to kill them."

"I heard that before."

"What are you…?"

"Pat Nelson said that, about Mrs. Jonsen, just a few minutes ago, when he was still alive. He didn't mean to kill her. Nobody meant to."

"I'm sure that's true. I'm sure it started out as a robbery and—"

"Go messing in mud and you're bound to get dirty, know what I mean, Lou? You go ripping people off and the damnedest things start happening."

"What are you saying, Mal?"

"You know what I'm saying."

And he did, too. He knew I'd finally pieced it together. Pieced together the factors, the odd factors that didn't seem to make sense until they were placed side by side. Like that, except for this one last-ditch robbery, all the break-ins had taken place outside the city limits in the sheriff's jurisdiction, where a deputy like Lou Brown would be privy to all sorts of information. And of course it was Lou who had taken the call from Pat Nelson the night Mrs. Jonsen was killed, that imaginary call that had supposedly reported the GTO stolen. And remember Lou questioning me that same night at the hospital coffee shop? Asking what my intentions were and then going straight to a phone—to check in with Brennan, he'd said, but in reality calling up Chet and Pat, who had gone over to my trailer to wait for me and further discourage me from poking around. And, too, Lou had graciously offered to keep me informed of Brennan's activities, while keeping track of what *I* was onto. Would I mind if he dropped in now and then? His folks were bugging him. Dropping in to misdirect me with false or at least wrongly slanted information, like his own reasoning behind why the break-ins were outside the city limits. He had given Pat the go-ahead with the keep-Mallory-busy scheme; after he'd ascertained yesterday afternoon that I was still set on looking into the break-ins, he had pretended to call his parents to let them know he wouldn't be home for supper, when he had actually been cuing Pat to have Debbie make her weepy phone call.

"Let me guess," I said. "The Petersens are long gone, am I right? Brennan's out there now, looking at nothing more than a deserted antique shop and barn. Because you had plenty of time to call the Petersens and tell them the heat was coming. So they've split, right?"

"I don't follow any of this."

"But when you called Tony's to warn your buddies, nobody was there but Felicia Richards. You didn't warn her, though, did you? Don't bother explaining why; I got that figured out, too. Only certain people knew about you, right, Lou? Only certain people knew about the inside man at the sheriff's office. Like the Petersens. And Chet. And Pat. But not P. J., huh? He's just a stooge. And not the women. Or the people you fence the goods through. Just the inner circle, the masterminds. Mastermind small-time, low-life punks like you, Lou."

"You better keep quiet, Mal. You don't know what you're getting into."

"Sure I do. So what happened, anyway? When you called Tony's and found nobody home but the woman, what did you do? Figure that they might try Mrs. Fox? Or were you listening to the police-band radio in your car? Or at the office? Oh, well. Doesn't matter. Probably none of it can be proved, anyway."

Under the pencil-line mustache, Lou's mouth formed a smile, just a little one.

"Because you tied up the loose ends, didn't you, Lou? You shot them. You blew 'em apart with your gun. You're really something, Lou. You're some goddamn friend in need. Indeed."

The sirens were starting now. Brennan would be here soon. Cops. Ambulance. In the background, people were watching us, Lou and me, watching a conversation they couldn't hear but wanted to. Morbid curiosity, it's called.

"I'll tell Brennan, of course. And he'll believe me. But I can't be sure it'll do any good. With the damn civil service the way it is, I don't even know if he can get away with firing you, let alone pressing charges. So you win, I guess. You ripped everybody off, and the spoils are yours. Have fun."

"I will," Lou said softly. "And I'm not worried. Because nobody's left."

He was right. The Petersens clearly had made it away before Brennan got there. Chet was dead. Pat was dead. P. J. knew nothing. The women knew nothing. Me? I had a patchwork quilt of guesses; try *that* out in court.

"I'm left," Debbie said.

We hadn't heard her come up behind us. I'm sure she hadn't wanted to leave Pat behind, but she'd felt the need to come over and join us. To let Lou know.

That she knew.

Husbands don't keep much from wives. Lou should have thought of that. And maybe Felicia Richards would turn out to know as much as Debbie. After all, Chet was her brother. Among other things.

Lou's hand tightened around the butt of the holstered .357 Magnum once again. Began to draw it out.

"Are you kidding?" I said. "Listen to those sirens. They're thirty seconds away. Look at all these people standing in their yards, on porches, watching. You going to shoot them, too? Get serious."

He let the gun drop back down in the holster.

He said, "I really didn't mean … want … to kill them. But it was all I could think of to do."

The tears came now. Debbie's, I mean. She buried her face in my chest, and I patted her head.

Lou touched his forehead with one hand and mumbled, "Damn sirens." He went over to the curb and sat and covered his ears with his hands, while the cars started rolling in on the scene: first cops, then ambulance, then Brennan, in close succession. Across from Lou, Pat and Chet were staring, empty-eyed. Lou was staring, too. With eyes just as empty.

25

I spent the next several weeks trying to forget the whole damn affair. I didn't have much luck. Every time I turned around, Brennan (who had become friendly due to the favorable publicity I'd helped him get) was stopping by to tell me the latest. I came to dread those visits, but also looked forward to them, since my desire to put the mess out of my mind was equaled by my natural curiosity to see how the details worked out. You might be curious, too, so I'll give you the nutshell version of what Brennan had to say.

While the Petersens had made it away that afternoon before Brennan could get out to their antique shop, they'd left a truck behind in their barn, a furniture truck with ramps set in back for the loaded green van to be driven up inside. The truck's place of purchase was traced to Cleveland, Ohio, where, not coincidentally, Lou Brown had been working in a factory until he decided to move back to Port City.

Brennan also said that a pattern involving the Petersens was forming, which should facilitate their eventual capture. Apparently, under various names, the couple had on at least four other occasions (in Georgia, Indiana, Ohio, and Illinois) made down-payments on down-at-the-mouth antique shops located out in the boonies, keeping up the payments for several months and then leaving town suddenly. The young couple skipping out after failing to make a go of their investment had never been remotely connected to the local outbreaks of breaking-and-entering. Now that it had, and the pattern was clear, it was just a matter of time, Brennan said, before the Petersens would join Lou Brown, whose trial was set to come up in three months.

My hunch about Felicia Richards was right; she, too, knew of Lou Brown's link to the break-in ring and was bitter enough about her brother's death to testify. The fact that doing so brought her immunity from prosecution may have had something to do with her cooperation. Because of such cooperation, neither Felicia nor Debbie was to be charged with anything.

Which was fine with me.

And now two weeks had gone by since the shooting out in front of Mrs. Fox's. I was getting back to my mystery novel and hoped to get the final draft typed up and in the mail by the middle of next month. And I had a good idea what my next one would be. Right now, however, I was drinking a Pabst, enjoying the solitude of my trailer. Didn't even have the stereo or TV on.

The phone rang, of course.

Solitude has a way of not lasting long—when I'm enjoying it, anyway.

"Mal? This is Debbie."

"I know. How are you doing?"

"Better. I haven't seen you since...."

"Right. You making the adjustment okay?"

"I suppose as well as can be expected. We're moved in with Mom now. A lot of our stuff was ... stolen property, you know, so all of that was confiscated. Cindy's taking it kind of hard. She was crazy about her daddy."

"Most little girls are. I'm sorry."

"Mal, I can't tell you what it means to me that you're not ... bitter about what ... what I did to you. I think about that—what I did—and it makes me feel so, God ... well, let's just say this wasn't an easy call to make."

"It wasn't a necessary one, either," I said. "I can understand what you did, without approving of it. Pat was your husband. You loved him. What you did came out of that."

"That's not completely true. We ... we really *were* unhappy. Pat wasn't a drunk, he didn't beat me; that was all a lie. But our lives weren't going anywhere. He couldn't keep a job. His job at the silo plant was the best he ever had, and he lost that for filching cases of Pepsi meant for the pop machine. That stuff I told you about him quitting was a cover-up. Pat was a kid—never grew up, still thought he could cheat and con and steal his way through life. But he didn't have it figured out, did he, Mal?"

"Have what figured out?"

"That when you take things from people, you take something from yourself, too." Silence for a moment. "Like me ripping you off, Mal. Emotionally. Like I have since we were kids." Silence again. "There are two really big rip-offs, Mal, the two biggest rip-offs of all. Know what they are?"

"No."

"One's death. Guess the other."

"I can't."

"It's life, silly."

"It doesn't have to be."

"I know that, Mal. It usually is, though, isn't it? Can I ask you something?"

"Debbie ... I really don't think seeing each other is a good idea."

"How do you know I was going to ask you to see me?"

"I just know."

"I'm glad you do, because … well, it started out with me lying to you, using you, to help Pat … but it became more than that, and I really did … *do* like you, Mal. Remember that morning you saw Sarah Petersen and me together at breakfast? Know what we were arguing about? I didn't want to do it anymore; didn't want to lie to you, use you, just couldn't stand doing that to you any longer."

"But you did."

"I did. I'm not strong, Mal. Neither was Pat. If I'd had somebody strong, it could've been different. You made me realize that, Mal. How things could've been different."

"They always could."

"Good-bye, Mal."

"Bye, Deb."

That conversation called for a fresh Pabst. I finished off the dregs of my present can and went for another. I got settled down to relax and couldn't get my mind empty, so I got up and put on a record album, a golden oldies record, hits from back in my junior high days. I listened to half a song, took it off, put on something newer.

And the phone rang again.

"Yes?"

"This is Edward Jonsen."

"What do you want, Jonsen?"

I had a good idea what he wanted. Several days ago I'd been contacted by the lawyer representing Mrs. Jonsen's estate. Seemed she'd made an addition to her will, codicil they call it, leaving all those Christmas plates to me. And the damn set of plates turned out to be even more valuable than Mrs. Jonsen had realized. The lawyer wouldn't give me their exact worth, but he did admit, "We're talking in the neighborhood of ten thousand dollars, Mr. Mallory." Which was a nice neighborhood.

Of course, Mrs. Jonsen had had plenty of other valuable antiques, and that fabled hidden loot of hers that Pat, Chet, and P. J. had searched so diligently for turned up in a bank safe-deposit box, and so Edward Jonsen was going to do all right even without the plates. But I'd made my mind up to give him the damn things anyway. What did I want with them? They'd just stir up memories I didn't want stirred, that's all. Let the fat bastard have the plates. Let him eat caviar off 'em; what did I care?

"Look, Jonsen, I've made a decision about those plates—"

"Don't bother asking for money, Mallory! I don't intend to pay you one cent for the plates. They are legally mine. I'm going to have that will broken; I've spoken to my attorney and he agrees with me. I'm going to fight this all the way; I can *prove* my mother was incompetent when she made that addition, I—"

I hung up.

Well, I supposed I could clear the movie posters off one wall and make room for the plates. Or maybe just sell them to some collector; my funds *were* getting kind of low. A mystery writer can always use a little extra cash, you know.

Edward Jonsen really did have more right to those plates than I, but some people just seem to deserve getting ripped off.

In the meantime, I had some hot suppers to deliver.

ABOUT THE AUTHOR

Max Allan Collins is the *New York Times* best-selling author of *Road to Perdition* and multiple award-winning novels, screenplays, comic books, comic strips, trading cards, short stories, movie novelizations, and historical fiction. He has scripted the *Dick Tracy* comic strip, *Batman* comic books, and written tie-in novels based on the *CSI*, *Bones*, and *Dark Angel* TV series; collaborated with legendary mystery author Mickey Spillane; and authored numerous mystery novels including the Quarry, Nolan, Mallory, and the bestselling Nathan Heller historical novels. His additional Mallory novels include *No Cure for Death*, *Kill Your Darlings*, *A Shroud for Aquarius*, and *Nice Weekend for a Murder*.

Made in the USA
Charleston, SC
23 November 2012